"Of course I believe you, Keith. Why would you lie?" Her voice danced with merriment.

"All right, Miss Know-it-all, I'll prove it to you. If Gretta will allow me to invade her domain one night, I'll make you a gourmet meal you'll never forget. And never again will you think to doubt the word of Keith Travers."

"You're on. But be warned—I intend to hold you to it. A night of grilled cheese sandwiches and soup might be nice for a change."

"Ha, ha—very funny. You'll see. I'll make you eat those words, Shae Stevens."

"Oh, but I'm sure they couldn't compare to your cooking talents, Keith. I'll just stick to food, thanks."

"I think what you need is a good spanking." He narrowed his eyes and steadily approached her. Giving a laughing yelp of protest, she dodged away and took off down the path. Keith gave chase. After letting her take the lead for a short time, he closed in and grabbed her arm. She squealed but didn't try to break away when he pulled her around to face him.

Out of breath, they stared at one another. Shae's face was rosy from running, and her eyes sparkled with a life of their own. Perspiration dotted her upper lip.

"You have jelly on the corner of your mouth," he panted, his voice low.

The tip of her tongue flicked to the purple spot, licking it away. His eyes stayed riveted to her mouth. He had never wanted to kiss anyone so badly. Forcing himself to look away, Keith pushed a shaky hand through his hair, sweeping it off his forehead. "I think we'd better head back."

PAMELA GRIFFIN lives in Texas and divides her time between family, church activities, and writing. She fully gave her life to the Lord Jesus Christ in 1988, after a rebellious young adulthood, and owes the fact that she's still alive today to an all-loving and forgiving God and to a mother who steadfastly prayed and had faith that God could bring her wayward daughter "home." Pamela's main goal in writing Christian romance is to help and encourage those who do know the Lord and to plant a seed of hope in those who don't. Pamela invites you to check out her web site: http://home.att.net/~words_of_honey/Pamela.htm

HEARTSONG PRESENTS

Books by Pamela Griffin
HP372—'Til We Meet Again
HP420—In the Secret Place

Angels to Watch over Me

Pamela Griffin

Heartsong Presents

Many thanks to my crit buds, Tracey B., Tamela H.M., Jill S., and Mom—for pitching in their time and effort at a moment's notice. You gals are the best! Also thanks to Lynn C. for answering my many questions, and to my pastor for his help.

I could have never written this without my Guardian and Lord, whose angels watched over this prodigal daughter, even when I wasn't aware of it.

A note from the author:
I love to hear from my readers! You may correspond with me by writing:

Pamela Griffin
Author Relations
PO Box 719
Uhrichsville, OH 44683

ISBN 1-58660-379-5

ANGELS TO WATCH OVER ME

All Scripture quotations, unless otherwise indicated, are taken from the HOLY BIBLE, NEW INTERNATIONAL VERSION®. NIV®. Copyright © 1973, 1978, 1984 by International Bible Society. Used by permission of Zondervan Publishing House. All rights reserved.

All of the characters and events in this book are fictitious. Any resemblance to actual persons, living or dead, or to actual events is purely coincidental.

Cover design by Lorraine Bush.

PRINTED IN THE U.S.A.

one

"Shae!"

Hearing the troubled voice of her young sister, Marcia "Shae" Stevens whipped her head sideways and lost her balance on the top platform of the stepladder where she precariously perched. She grabbed for one of the nearby shelves and just prevented herself from toppling to the floor.

"Tiffany! What's wrong?" Shae tightened her fingers around the feather duster in her other hand and studied the guilt-ridden faces of her sister and her sister's best friend and accomplice, Liz Reihlander. Shae glanced at the chubby redhead, whose gaze seemed permanently fixed on the polished planks of the wooden floor, then looked back to her fourteen-year-old sister, Tiffany.

Tiffany's eyes darted nervously around the storage room, flicking only briefly to Shae before flying away again. Shae's heart began to beat faster with dread.

Oh, what mischief had the two cooked up this time?

"I gotta go. My mom said I had to be home by five." Liz turned and fled the room.

Tiffany's eyes followed her, as if she'd been betrayed.

"Okay, Tiff, let's have it." Shae tried to keep her voice controlled. She had learned long ago that blowing up after hearing Tiffany's confessions from past shenanigans had done nothing but cause more problems. After taking the three steps down the ladder, Shae looked to Tiffany's hand, which tightly clutched a piece of yellow paper. "Is that for me?"

Tiffany bit her lip, hazel eyes widening with apprehension. "We were only having a little fun. We never thought anything like this would really happen. Honest!"

"The paper, Tiffany."

Reluctantly, Tiffany handed her the soiled and crumpled note. At a glance Shae could see it was a business telegram.

Miss Stevens,
  We are pleased to inform you that you have won the contest for "A Dream Date with Keith Travers" spon- sored by Teen Planet Magazine. *We will contact you on the twentieth of this month to discuss the arrangements.*

Sincerely,
Frederick W. Smith
Star Artists Management

Shae barely quenched the smile threatening to take over her mouth as she scanned the paper. She fingered the hole at the bottom of her worn plaid flannel shirt, wondering how to deal with this new development. It wouldn't do for her to treat the matter too lightly. Tiffany got away with far too much as it was.

"A little young to be going on a date with Keith Travers, aren't you, Tiffany?" Shae said in what she hoped was a formi- dable tone of voice. "Well, you'll just have to call and tell them it was all a big mistake and you're sorry."

Tiffany's rosy color faded until it matched the flocked ivory petunias on the pine green wallpaper. With growing alarm, Shae's hand tightened on the letter. "There's more you're not telling me, isn't there?"

"We entered your name in the contest!" Tiffany blurted. "You had to be at least eighteen to enter."

The blood drained from Shae's face. The faint trace of amusement she'd felt at the childish prank disappeared as swiftly as a wave crashing on the beach and receding into the sea. She remembered how insistent the girls had been about taking her picture months ago with Liz's new camera. "That's why you took the pictures of me by the ocean?"

"Yes, but—oh, Shae. . ."

"There's more?" Shae asked, eyes flying wide with disbelief.

"The pictures, uh. . .they didn't turn out. And there wasn't time to take more. So we, um. . .we sent one in of Samantha."

"Now let me get this straight." Shae put a hand to a forehead that was beginning to throb. "You entered my name and Samantha's picture in a contest for a date with Keith Travers—the famous recording artist—and now you've found out you won?"

Tiffany nodded miserably. "And we also had to write and tell them about your hobbies and other stuff."

"Great! Just what I needed, Tiffany!" Shae threw down the feather duster and marched out of the room, her younger sister following like a whipped puppy. "Well, you'll just have to get on the phone and—wait a minute! What was the date on that note?"

Remembering she still gripped the yellow paper, Shae brought it up to her eyes and let out a horrified gasp. "The twentieth—that's today! Oh, Tiff. Why didn't you give this to me earlier? You probably got this before today, didn't you?"

Tiffany gave a reluctant nod.

"I thought so. You've really landed a whopper this time. I only hope it's not too late to call—though it's strange they haven't confirmed the date yet. Their office hours should be over soon," Shae rambled, her panicked thoughts tumbling from her mouth.

She had to think clearly, stay in control, stay on top of things and not let this new mountain topple on her head. "Do you have the number to reach them? No? Well then, we'll have to call information first, since all we have is their address. I want you to know, Tiffany Lauren Stevens—this is coming out of your allowance!"

Shae rubbed dirty hands on equally dirty jeans and reached for the phone. Tiffany slumped against the wall next to the curved receiving desk, faint wrinkles creasing her brow. Shae punched a few buttons and waited for an operator to come on the line. After reaching the state and city she needed, she took a calming breath.

"Los Angeles Directory Assistance? Yes, please. I'd like the number of Star Artists. . ."

The brisk wind sneaked in and toyed with papers and tourist guides on the polished oak counter as the front door to the inn opened. Two men walked inside, one wearing dark sunglasses despite the overcast day.

"Never mind, Operator," Shae managed in a small voice. "Thank you." Dropping the humming receiver into its cradle, she eyed the newcomers with dread. She would have recognized the taller of the two anywhere. After all, his glossy likeness was plastered on her sister's wall.

His dark-spectacled gaze briefly looked her over and just as quickly dismissed her. He scanned the old-fashioned room, a look of boredom on his handsome features. The shorter man walked to where Shae stood clutching the edge of the counter with white-knuckled fingers. Balding and fat, he studied her with piggish eyes, an unlit cigar stuck in his mouth. "We're looking for the home of Shae Stevens. This is the address we were given."

Shae swallowed, trying to find her voice. "I. . .I'm sorry." The words came out in a high-pitched squeak, and she cleared her throat. "I'm afraid there's been a mistake."

She darted a look at Tiffany, who'd been inching her way backward out of the room with wide eyes pinned to Keith Travers. Tiffany caught Shae's warning gaze and wilted against the wainscoting.

"This isn't the home of Shae Stevens?" Bald Man asked sharply. Keith stopped his disinterested study of the antique furnishings and joined the other man at the arched counter.

"Um, no. I–I mean, yes," Shae stammered, strongly aware of Keith's dark gaze planted on her. "But. . .well, the fact is you've been led here under false pretenses. I'm really sorry. I–I was trying to call just now and tell you. . .I only just found out about all this. . .but I had no idea you'd come here. . . ."

"We'd like to discuss this with Miss Stevens. I assume you work for her," Bald Man said critically, eyeing her casual attire.

"Um, no. Actually, I am her. . .I mean she's me." She gave a nervous little laugh that held no humor. "I'm Shae Stevens."

"What!" He pulled a photograph from the inside pocket of his business suit. Shae caught a glimpse of the gorgeous blue-eyed, blond Samantha Reihlander.

"You're Shae Stevens?"

Keith Travers's baritone voice was rich, like creamy cappuccino. He slowly pulled off designer sunglasses, and it was all Shae could do not to gape as his piercing blue eyes studied her. Pictures definitely didn't do this man justice.

Opting for levity in the midst of this nightmare being played out by the four of them, Shae offered a wobbly smile. "Last time I looked, that was my name."

❧

Frowning, Keith took in the smooth olive complexion devoid of makeup. Dirt smudged one high cheekbone and her forehead. A blue bandanna covered her hair, and only by the wisps that had escaped near her temple could he tell she was a brunette. A pair of silver-rimmed wire glasses sat perched on her slightly upturned nose, and through them he saw thickly-lashed, almond-shaped dark eyes—wide and staring.

He bunched his brows. "Is this some kind of joke? You're a little old to be playing games like this, aren't you? And certainly too old to be reading teen magazines, I'd think."

She visibly stiffened. "I assure you, Mr. Travers, this wasn't my idea, but rather the mischief of two young girls who've had way too much time on their hands. I promise you they'll be properly dealt with." While addressing him, she darted a glance toward the teen hugging the wall. "I hope this little misunderstanding hasn't inconvenienced you too much. Please believe me when I say I'm sorry."

Intermingled feelings of interest and curiosity swamped Keith when he saw the quivering, stuttering girl had disappeared to be replaced by a self-assured woman with a fiery sparkle in her chocolate-colored eyes.

"Inconvenienced! Lady, you have no idea—"

"Let it go, Freddie." Keith stopped his manager's beginning tirade with an upraised hand. His glance went to the trembling girl who looked as if she'd gladly melt into the wall if given the chance. Except for the eyes, she was a replica of Shae. He could pretty well guess what had happened. Little sister played a prank on big sister. How often had he and his older brother caused pandemonium in his family's lives with similar escapades?

"We accept your apology."

"We do?" Freddie looked at Keith in stunned disbelief. "I mean—yeah, sure. We do."

"Oh, I'm so relieved!" Shae gave them a dazzling smile. Keith noted even her face and eyes seemed to light up from within.

Freddie grumbled something and turned from the counter. "Come on, Travers. We gotta get back to California and look through the entries again. I had a feeling all along it was a mistake to accept a winner from the East Coast. Only cold and fog, fog and cold—can't expect nothin' more from a place like this. Next time the winner is coming to us, like is always done in these kinds of contests. But no-o-o-o—you had to change all the rules and fly all the way out here. . . ." His complaints trailed off as he stomped out the door.

"Don't mind him," Keith said. "He's been a bear ever since he quit smoking."

"Under the circumstances, I'd say more like a teddy bear. Thank you both for being so understanding."

"Believe me, Miss Stevens, I understand more than you think I do." His gaze lighted on Tiffany, and he gave her a smile and a wink. "Bye, now."

Now what did he mean by that?

Puzzled, Shae forced her gaze away from the door the singer had exited and looked at Tiffany. Stars shone in the teen's eyes, all former anxiety seeming to have vanished. "Oh, Shae, did you see that? Keith Travers actually smiled at me. . .and he winked at me too! I'll never forget this day as long as I live. . . ."

Pulling her mouth into a severe frown, Shae crossed her arms and stared at her swooning sister. "You certainly won't, young lady. Thanks to Mr. Travers's generosity, things went a lot better than I expected. But that doesn't excuse the fact that you lied and interfered in other people's lives."

Tiffany gave no indication she'd heard, her expression showing she was still in la-la land.

Shae let out a weary sigh. "As of this moment you're grounded for two weeks—make that a month. And you can spend that time helping out at the inn instead of loafing around and dreaming up more mischief. You can start by helping Gretta in the kitchen. Right now—go."

Tiffany glided toward the designated area, the dreamy smile still on her face. Not even Shae's sharp words or the reality of being grounded seemed to have any effect on her at the moment. Shae watched as her sister walked smack into the wooden door frame.

She shook her head. Raising a younger sibling, especially a teenaged girl, was harder than she had assumed it would be. Had she been so hard to control when she'd been Tiffany's age?

Instant heaviness settled over Shae like a suffocating shroud, as memory taunted. Escape. She needed escape. Rushing up the stairs to her room, she ripped the bandanna from her head. Maybe a good jog in the brisk sea air would be just the thing.

She tore out the mammoth-sized hair clasp, brushed her thick mass of hair, and secured it with a rubber band. After changing into a pine green sweat suit, she pulled on a pair of high-topped sneakers and a windbreaker. Studying her reflection, she wiped away the dirt with a tissue. Huge eyes stared back through the lenses of her glasses, looking vulnerable and uncertain. The men's earlier appraisal made her feel that she'd been found wanting. And for some reason, that bothered her.

Though she wasn't vain, Shae had always tried to look her best around others, and to be caught looking like such a mess, and by Keith Travers to boot, had given her feminine ego—what little of it there was—quite a jolt. She knew Keith was considered a heartthrob to many of her gender—teenagers and women alike. And who wouldn't wonder? What with those unbelievably bright blue eyes of his and that wheat blond hair waving about his neck, almost touching his collarbone. . .not to mention that million-dollar smile. . . .

"Marcia Shae Stevens—stop it right now!" she angrily confronted her reflection. "You're no better than those mooney-eyed teenagers. What would your mother say?" A haunted look came into the dark eyes staring back.

Yes. . .what would Mother say?

She backed up, turned, and fled the room. Darting down the stairs, out the door, and into the cloudy day, she ran as if racing the wind while trying to escape the ghosts of her past.

❧

After a good brisk run, Shae returned to the inn feeling better. Yet once she opened the door she knew her improved disposition wasn't meant to last.

Hillary Collins paced the polished wooden floor, her high heels only silenced as they passed over wide Oriental scatter rugs. Catching sight of Shae, she stopped. Shae could see in a moment that Hillary had been crying, and heavily. Her face was blotchy, her eyes red.

"Is it Robert?" Shae asked softly, moving to stand beside the distraught woman.

Hillary nodded. "Oh, Shae. He's in jail!" She practically collapsed against her, throwing thin arms around her shoulders.

Relieved to see the front desk empty of curious onlookers, Shae shepherded Hillary into the office. After helping her friend onto a cushioned chair, Shae closed the door. "Tell me."

"He got pulled over for a DUI on the mainland." Hillary sniffled. "He must have gotten belligerent—you know how he can be when he's been drinking. Ever since I became a Christian last winter, his drinking has gotten worse. Oh, Shae. . .I just don't know what to do anymore!" She broke down into a fresh torrent of tears.

Shae sighed. Robert and Hillary were the inn's floor show. Robert played the piano, and his wife sang. Shae had known about his drinking problem, but he usually kept it under control and didn't let it affect his performances.

Hillary lifted smudged eyes to Shae. "Will you pray with me, Shae? Please?"

"Of course," Shae murmured, though she wasn't sure it would do any good. The possibility of her prayers being heard was slim. Yet she wanted to help her friend, and God might listen since the request didn't involve Shae.

She took Hillary's cold hands and offered a shaky prayer, hoping Hillary couldn't tell how rusty she was. Afterward, she opened her eyes, affecting a small smile. "Don't worry about tonight. I'll find a replacement. You go and get Robert out of jail. Do you need bail money?"

"Well, I did just pay rent and a few other bills. But I can't take your money, Shae. I'll get the rest somehow. . . ." Her voice dwindled away, uncertain, scared.

Shae ignored her and went to the wall safe. "How much more do you need?"

"The bail bondsman said it would take a thousand—but I only need to pay 10 percent up front."

Shae's eyebrows went up at Hillary's meek answer, but then again it wasn't Robert's first time in jail. She fiddled with the knob and opened the door to the safe, pulling a few bills from the padded, zippered case inside. "You're lucky I haven't gone to the bank yet. Here. No, I insist. Take it. I'm not in lack, and you need it right now. You can pay me back when you're able."

"Thank you. I don't know where we'd be without you." Hillary's voice sounded relieved and tortured at the same time.

"I think our paths crossed for a reason, Hillary. God takes care of His own, you know." These last words came out wooden, learned by rote, but Hillary didn't seem to notice. Shae quickly slammed the door of the safe.

"You're right, Shae. And I believe you're my own guardian angel He sent to watch out for me." Still teary-eyed, Hillary took the proffered bills with a grateful smile and hug, then left the office. Her soft words resounded in Shae's ears, mocking her.

And what angel had looked out for her parents that night over seven years ago? Where had God been when they needed Him? But then—the disaster hadn't been God's fault. The blame was hers. All hers.

Shae sank onto her chair and dropped her forehead into her hands. Was God standing in the clouds, angry and waiting to bang a huge, deserved anvil on her head?

She attended her local church because she knew it was required of a Christian. She said and did what she thought was right, helped others, never broke the Ten Commandments. . . Still Shae had little hope that heaven would one day be her eternal home. But the thought of going to hell terrified her. She visited it each night in her dreams. . . .

With an angry, muffled exclamation, she straightened and snatched up the slim telephone book at her elbow to scan its pages for a replacement act. Things were certainly bad enough in the present without dwelling on the past. Or the future.

❧

"You've gotta be kidding! It's important we get back to LA as soon as possible." Freddie's face reddened as he chewed on the stump of his unlit cigar.

"Sorry, Mister. Fog's too thick. Won't be going anywhere 'til it clears. Too dangerous."

Both Keith and Freddie looked out at the wall of dense white fog smothering an unusually calm ocean and heading in their direction. "There must be someone with a boat who's willing to try it. I'd pay them well."

The old sailor crossed his arms and wryly observed them

from eyes the color of the sea. "Not likely you'd find anyone round these parts. Old Man McClury's got a rowboat. But he wouldn't risk it. Too smart. He might be willing to rent it out to you. But you'd be on your own."

Freddie let out a harsh expletive. Even Keith was getting irritated with the crusty boatman's sarcasm. No one in his right mind would take a small rowboat over twelve miles of foggy ocean.

"Listen, Freddie," Keith said, "your ranting and raving isn't helping any. We might as well face it—we're stuck here for the night. I vote we head back to that inn and see if there are any vacancies. I'm beat."

"We should've taken the ferry," Freddie mumbled. "At least then we'd be on the mainland now."

"Ferries don't run in fog," the boatman shot back. "Planes either."

"Yeah, so we heard." After throwing a nasty look at the unruffled local, Freddie turned to Keith. "Let's find a telephone book and call a taxi."

Keith nodded, relieved Freddie had finally given in. They had chartered a flight from Providence, but the planes at the small island airport were now grounded due to the oncoming bad weather. Unfortunately, they'd left their overnight bags in an airport locker on the mainland. Chartering a small boat had been Freddie's last-ditch effort to get there.

Once the cab arrived, Freddie slid beside Keith on the backseat, grumbling something about New England's lousy weather and being trapped on a remote island. Yet Keith was relieved at this turn of events. He wasn't ready for more wearying hours of travel yet, having recently completed a concert tour, and would enjoy a short break on Block Island. Besides, he had other interests in this part of the country—that is, if he didn't lose his nerve. Interests Freddie knew nothing about.

Soon they again found themselves in front of the renovated Victorian inn—one of many scattered throughout the island's lone city of New Shoreham. They took the four steps to the wraparound porch of the three-story building that boasted dark gray siding and white gingerbread trim. In the old-fashioned lobby, a young girl with a blond ponytail checked them in and gave them their room keys, all the while casting surreptitious glances at Keith. "Say, Mister, did you know you look a lot like—"

"Yeah, Kid. He hears it all the time," Freddie interrupted. "Is there a dining room in this joint?"

The blond nodded. "Down that hall and to your left. You're just in time for the floor show."

"Whoopee."

At Freddie's sardonic reply, the girl stared, clearly puzzled.

"Lighten up, Freddie," Keith muttered under his breath.

Following her directions, they found themselves in a large room with a stage against one wall and linen-covered square tables in front. Stubby candles glowed from within smoky, netted glass globes on the center of each table. The dark wooden decor looked as if it would fit right in a hundred years previously, except for the dim lights glowing from strategic places along the high-beamed ceiling. Long picture windows covered one side, giving a view of the fog-covered ocean.

"Charming," Freddie drawled.

"Will you cut it out already? We're stuck here, so we might as well make the most of it." Keith surveyed the large room, hoping to catch a glimpse of Shae Stevens. The no-frills woman intrigued him, though he couldn't begin to understand why. She was nothing like the glamour girls he knew.

They sat at a back table in the corner, so the small crowd of diners wouldn't easily notice them. A middle-aged woman wearing a navy uniform ambled their way with menus. The two men scanned the plastic covers, made their order, and the waitress bustled away.

"Only five choices for entrées? Say what kind of place is this?" Freddie complained to his dinner partner. "And I didn't see any alcohol on the menu. Don't tell me everyone around here is a teetotaler."

"Shh. The floor show is about to begin," Keith said as a lovely young woman took the stage, moved toward the piano, and sat on the matching bench.

The overhead lights went out, and a blue spotlight beamed down on her. The woman's waist-length hair shone a glossy blue-black, swaying gently to and fro, as her slim hands began to roam the ivory keys. Her winter-white dress sparkled in the light.

Keith studied her over his lowered sunglasses a moment, then resumed scanning the dim room. Judging from her appearance, Shae Stevens was probably a maid and wouldn't be working in the dining room, but one never knew.

The woman at the piano began to sing, and Keith's attention again turned her way. He noticed even Freddie perked up. She sang a few show tunes from the forties and fifties, her soft voice ringing with a clear bell-like quality. The last note from a sad love song barely died away before Freddie turned to Keith, an excited gleam in his eye.

"Maybe it's not such a bad thing we got stuck here after all, Travers," he said over the burst of loud clapping in the room. "We've been looking for a replacement backup singer for your new CD. She's perfect. Understated—yet the lady can carry a tune and then some. And she definitely has stage presence. Whattaya think?"

Keith, who was often skeptical of Freddie's ideas, nodded slowly. *Yes, she could fill Lil's shoes. Providing she was willing, of course.* He watched as she stood, acknowledged the audience's applause with a graceful bow and hurried backstage.

Freddie shot to his feet. "Come on. Let's find her before she gets away."

"But we haven't eaten yet!"

"You can eat later. We don't want to lose her."

"Freddie, I haven't eaten since this morning. . . ."

But Keith spoke to empty air. His manager was already three tables away and heading for the door. With a frustrated groan, Keith snatched up his water glass and downed its contents, then plucked two large wheat rolls from the basket the waitress had set on the table before writing down their order. Taking a huge bite of one roll, he stood and followed Freddie.

After searching a few of the public rooms, they again found themselves at the reception counter, the same blond again giving Keith the eye while he finished off his last roll.

"We'd like to speak to the lady who sang for the floor show," Freddie said.

The blond chewed her lip. "I guess that would be Hillary Collins, but I thought I saw her leave earlier. Short blond hair, deep sultry voice?"

"No, no, no!" Freddie bellowed. "The lady had long dark hair and a sweet voice that could charm the birds from the trees."

"But. . .I'm sorry. I. . .I don't know who—"

Freddie let out a few choice words. "Don't you even know who you hire for your entertainment?"

"I only work here p–part-time." The girl's lip quivered and her eyes filled with tears. Keith was about to admonish Freddie, when a familiar voice spoke from behind.

"Is there a problem, Katie?"

The girl's eyes widened. "Miss Stevens."

The men turned simultaneously. Keith's jaw dropped as he came face-to-face with Shae and realized she was the girl for whom they'd been searching. From their back table, Keith hadn't been able to see her clearly. Yet even if he would have had a front row seat, center stage, he doubted he would've recognized her.

Her face was dramatically made up—minus the glasses—smoky blue enhancing dark eyes that sparkled like black star sapphires. Pink blusher swept the high cheekbones, and her lips were a bright cherry red. Blue-black hair fell in a dark curtain to her waist.

A white lace dress hugged her slim curves, and a scalloped, straight neckline barely revealed the tips of her round shoulders. Sprinkled with rhinestones, the dress caught the light and matched the sparkle in her eyes. A choker of tiny white diamonds encircled her neck, and matching earrings dangled from her ears.

Keith blinked, stunned. *She looks like a bride.* And then, remarkably, it was as if the present faded away and she was standing amid myriad colorful flowers beside the ocean, wearing another white dress and looking up at him with eyes of love—as if she'd become his bride. . . .

He shook his head to clear it. What was wrong with him? Was he hallucinating? Unlike some in his profession, he didn't do drugs—though he had tampered with them the first two and a half years of his career. An episode he now regretted, as he did so many other events in his life. Still, his former drug abuse and drinking didn't explain how he could be seeing things that weren't there now.

The day had been long and filled with surprises. Maybe he was just tired and hungry. Definitely hungry. He turned to Freddie and tried to concentrate on what his manager was saying.

"So you're the nightingale. Hmm. . . Tell me, Miss Stevens, besides acting as a maid, a desk clerk, and entertainment for this inn, what other duties do you perform?"

"What?" She blinked, evidently still as flustered as Keith, and turned her gaze away from him to Freddie.

"I asked what you do here."

"Oh. I own and manage The Roosting Place. I was on my way to my room to change when I heard the commotion." Her words sounded nervous as she looked at Keith. "I must say I'm surprised to see you again, Mr. Travers. I didn't expect you back."

Katie let out a squeal. "Then you are Keith Travers—I knew it! Wait 'til Amber hears about this. And you're staying here for the night—Keith Travers is staying at The Roosting Place!"

Shae lifted her brow in surprise, and he nodded. "The fog trapped us."

She turned toward the desk. "Katie, not a word of this to

anyone while these men are our guests. Is that understood?"

Katie nodded grudgingly, never taking her eyes off Keith, who still looked at Shae.

"Have you eaten yet, Miss Stevens?" Freddie asked after a moment, a smug note to his voice.

"No."

"Good. Maybe you'd like to eat with us then? We have some business we'd like to discuss. Don't we, Travers? *Travers!*"

"Huh?" Keith forced himself to look away. Freddie was smiling that Cheshire cat grin and had that all too familiar gleam in his eye. Keith held back a groan. Knowing his manager, this didn't look good.

two

As they neared the dining room, Shae moved in the opposite direction. "Tiffany and I usually take our meals privately." She stopped and looked at them. "Unless, of course, you'd prefer to eat in the dining room?"

"No, no. Lead the way, Miss Stevens. Wherever you usually eat is fine with us," Freddie almost crooned.

Shae continued down the hall and opened a door. "This is it."

She almost laughed aloud at his expression when they entered a kitchen. He'd obviously been expecting a little more grandeur, to say the least. A rotund, middle-aged woman stood over the industrial-sized stove, stirring something in a huge pot. She smiled at them and nodded, then turned back to her work.

"This is Gretta, one of the best cooks on the island, as I'm sure you'll soon agree. I know all of Germany must miss her delicious strudels. Gretta, these are our guests: Mr. Smith and Mr. Travers," Shae said, inclining her head toward each man as she gave the introductions.

Gretta's ears turned red from the compliments, but she smiled and nodded. *"Guten abend.* Please, you must sit down and I will serve you, *ja?"*

Shae led them past an accordion screen that acted as a partition in secluding a room for dining. Tiffany sat at the table, a forkful of sauerkraut halfway to her mouth. She raised her head to see who'd joined her. The fork fell with a loud clatter to her plate. Her eyes widened, saucer-like, a stupefied expression covering her face.

"Tiffany, you remember Mr. Travers and Mr. Smith. They're our guests at The Roosting Place tonight."

"They're staying here!" Tiffany squeaked.

Shae ignored her, turning to the men. "And this, as I'm sure you've probably guessed by now, is one of the girls responsible for your coming east. My sister Tiffany."

Keith pocketed his sunglasses and moved to stand in front of the girl, taking her limp hand in a gentle handshake. "It's a pleasure to meet you, Tiffany."

Tiffany stared at the hand he'd held as if she'd never seen it before, then up into his eyes. Shae was afraid Tiffany would faint any moment, as goofy as she was acting.

"Tiff, if you're finished with dinner, you'd better head upstairs and start your homework. I seem to remember something you said about a science report being due Friday. We three have some business to discuss—"

"Oh! Then you're going to do it!" Tiffany straightened in her chair, a smile beaming across her face.

"Do what?"

"You're going on a date with him after all—even if you don't look like Samantha. Wait 'til I tell Liz!"

Shae's face suffused with heat. "Tiffany, I—"

"Yes, she is, Tiffany. And if you want the truth," Keith leaned down conspiratorially toward the gawking teenager, "I think she's much cuter than Samantha."

Shae looked at him, dumbfounded, her face growing even hotter. "I am?"

"Yes. You're really quite pretty."

"No, no! I mean, I'm going on a date with you?"

Tiffany squealed with delight. "Great—it worked! Liz said it would, but I wasn't sure after what happened today."

"What are you talking about?" Shae demanded.

"Nothing. I'd better go do my homework." She pushed away from the table. "Night, Shae! Night, Mr. Travers!" she called back in a singsong voice, miraculously shedding her awkwardness with Keith like a snake sheds its skin.

"Tiffany!" But she was already out the door. Shae whirled to face Keith. "Really! I wish you wouldn't have encouraged her. She's impossible as it is. You shouldn't have told her that."

"Why not? You did win the contest."

"But. . .that was under false pretenses. You thought I was Samantha, remember? Besides, I don't date."

Keith's brows lifted in surprise. "Why not?"

"Because I. . .well, I—"

"Look, it's just one date. There'll be a reporter along acting as chaperon. He has to write the story for the teen magazine that started the contest in the first place. And there'll be a photographer there too."

"A photographer?" Shae swallowed, trying not to panic. Years had elapsed since those days. No one would recognize her now.

"Yeah, all part of the publicity. Not that any part of this contest was my idea, mind you," Keith added dryly, his gaze cutting to Freddie before capturing hers again. "But if this date has to be, I'd rather it be with you than anyone else. Please say you'll reconsider."

Shae blinked. Was this a dream? Was the famous Keith Travers actually begging her for a date? It must be a dream. Reality wasn't this fantastic. "Well, perhaps just one date wouldn't hurt. . . ."

Keith's smile grew wide, sending shock waves to her heart. Or would it?

"*Ach,* sit down, sit down." Gretta hustled in with steaming platters of sauerkraut and sausages. "Why are you just standing there, staring at one another across the table?"

Shae and Keith exchanged embarrassed smiles and sat. Freddie also pulled up a chair. Automatically, Shae bowed her head in prayer. "For what we are about to receive, Lord, we are truly thankful. Amen."

Lifting her eyes, realizing what she'd just done, Shae was shocked to see Keith gazing at her, his expression soft. A scowl covered Freddie's lined face.

Diving into his food, he began, "I told you there was some business we wanted to discuss with you, Miss Stevens. We've been looking for a backup—"

"Another time, Freddie," Keith broke in. "It can wait 'til tomorrow. Let's not bring up business now." He took a heaping bite of sauerkraut. "Hey, this is good!"

Opening his mouth again, Freddie stared at Keith. The singer shook his head, his eyes issuing a warning, making Shae wonder.

Freddie closed his mouth, his brows pulled down in a scowl. "Sure, okay, swell. We'll talk in the morning."

❧

Not long after the sun had risen above the ocean, while eating a breakfast of white cornmeal johnnycakes, crisp bacon, scrambled eggs, and apple strudel, Freddie dove into the subject with as much relish as he dove into his food. "Miss Stevens, we have something we'd like to discuss with you, concerning a job. . . ."

Exasperated, Keith discreetly waved one hand at table level and shook his head, trying to get his manager's attention. Freddie ignored him and forked up another helping of egg.

"One of Travers's backup singers will soon be leaving the band," he said, mouth full. "We've been searching for someone to take her place, and after hearing your performance last night, we think you would work out."

"You were there?" Shae's voice was a mere whisper, and Keith wondered if Freddie noticed how wide her eyes had gone.

"Yes, we saw the whole thing. You have an adequate voice, Miss Stevens, and with a little work we think you could fit in—"

Shae awkwardly stood, knocking her leg against the back of the chair, almost toppling it over. "No thank you, Mr. Smith. I'm really not interested. Excuse me."

Throwing down her napkin, she made her escape—there was no other word to describe it. As though she were a prisoner who'd just realized the guard's back was turned and the shackles were loose.

Frustrated, Keith turned to Freddie, "Why'd you have to open your big mouth? I was trying to tell you to stop."

"Who'd have known she'd react like that? You'd have thought I had offered her sister's head to her on a platter the way she ran outta here. And did you see the look in her eyes? What's with her?"

"I'm not sure. But I had an idea something like this would happen from the way she acted last night when we brought up the contest. One reason I would have preferred to talk to her about the job myself." Keith sighed, his gaze briefly going to the door through which she'd exited. "I think where Shae Stevens is concerned we're going to have to tread lightly."

"Well, I don't like it." Freddie's expression turned grim. "I'll admit, at first I was glad that you'd finally found someone who interested you." He held up his hand to stop Keith's automatic denial. "Yes, she does—don't feed me any lines. I've seen that look in other men's eyes before, usually before they head for the altar. Like I said, at first I thought 'why not?' Other artists have taken the plunge, and it hasn't affected the sales of their CDs or the amount of concert tickets sold."

"I don't want to talk about this right now," Keith said, annoyed.

"Hear me out, Travers." Freddie leaned forward. "It's bothered me that you haven't shown any interest in a woman for a long time—it's not good for your image. Except for the publicity dates I arrange, you pretty much stay to yourself."

Keith didn't answer. The women he'd been associated with weren't exactly marriage material.

"But with this Shae character," Freddie continued, "I just don't know. She's one weird dame. You don't suppose she's wanted by the law and is hiding out on this island?" Freddie stabbed another forkful of egg and held it horizontally, propping his elbow on the table. He shook the fork. "It makes sense, ya know. Rhode Island is the smallest state in the country, and this is certainly one of the littlest islands I ever saw. What better place for a hideout?"

Keith gave a disbelieving snort, but Freddie pensively went on as if he hadn't heard him.

"Maybe she killed off her husband and is afraid someone will recognize her. Or maybe she's had several and killed them all—like that movie I saw last week. She seems to be loaded. That's probably where she got the dough. And that would also explain why she's so nervous about dating—she doesn't want it to happen again—"

"Or maybe the *real* problem is that you watch too many of those brain-warping psycho-flicks," Keith responded dryly. He gave Freddie a disgusted look and rose from the table. "I'm going out for some air."

Keith found Shae on the front porch, the salty, cold breeze blowing tendrils into her face, despite the fact that a red velvet band held back her hair. He sank to the top step beside her. Whitecaps ruffled the grayish blue sea, the waves giving a loud hiss as they hit the beach. Wispy clouds, like trailing strips of gauze, floated in a pale blue sky.

"Sorry about the way I acted in there," she said, staring out over the expanse of water.

"You have my manager really worried. He's now convinced you're a psychopathic killer who's just bumped off another wealthy husband and is afraid of being discovered."

Shae's head zipped his way, her eyes widening. She laughed, though Keith thought it held a nervous ring. "And how did he reach that conclusion?"

"You don't know Freddie. Once he lets that imagination of his start to work, watch out!" He studied her profile when she didn't answer. "I wouldn't worry about it. He's harmless."

She absentmindedly nodded, and they passed a few moments in silence, staring at the view.

"Bumping off wealthy husbands, huh?" She gave a dry chuckle. "If I liked to tease I might have fun with that."

"Maybe you should. It's about time someone put Freddie in his place." Relieved that her mood had lightened, Keith took a chance. "You know, you really do have a beautiful voice. Can you tell me why you're not interested in being my backup singer?"

Instantly she stiffened. Afraid she would bolt again, he quickly added, "It's okay if you don't want to. I shouldn't have brought it up a second time."

She lowered her lashes. "Please don't take this wrong, Mr. Travers, but I don't really care for today's music."

"I see." Sensing there was more, he asked, "And is that the only reason?"

Shae kept her gaze on her hands. "Yes."

Her word came out faint, and Keith was sure she was holding something back. "Okay." He let out a weary breath. Strike two. "So, where would you like to go for our date?"

"What?" That got her attention.

"Anything special you'd like to do for our date?"

Her face matched her dusky-rose sweater. "You mean *we* choose? I thought the magazine staff would arrange everything."

"No. Nothing specific was made out. Just a contest for a date—that's all. Normally the magazine's PR rep would have contacted you, but Freddie insisted on screening the winner, and he usually gets his way. Not always, though. Once or twice I've had something to say about it."

Shae tilted her head, lines of confusion marring her brow. "If he believes I'm a psychopath, what makes you think he'll let me go on a date with you?"

Keith chuckled. "I wouldn't worry about it. Like I said— once in awhile I get the final word. And I happen to think you're pretty normal."

She nodded, looked away.

"So, is there anything special you'd like to do? Rent a yacht, or go sailing maybe? Then dinner at a nice restaurant or something like that? Or we could do something on the mainland if you'd prefer."

"I'd like to think about it. When would the date take place?"

"Tomorrow too soon?"

Shae's eyes widened and her mouth opened in shocked protest.

"Just kidding." Keith grinned, leaning back on his elbows.

"Freddie will have to make arrangements with *Teen Planet* to send a reporter and photographer. It probably would be next week at the earliest. Okay with you?"

"I think so. The inn practically runs itself, what with all the help I have. The only problems I've had lately concern the floor show—but I'm usually able to find a replacement. Last night was the first time I couldn't—not enough advance notice."

"You mean you don't usually perform?"

"No."

The reply was clipped, and Keith noted the shuttered look that slammed over her face. Again, he decided to change the subject. "I guess we'll be staying on your island awhile. I sure could use the vacation. Can you board us?"

"Of course. There are plenty of rooms and few reservations—tourist season doesn't really start for a few weeks yet. But, Mr. Travers—"

"Call me Keith. If we're going to be dating, it would seem strange for you to call me anything else."

"Uh, Keith," she said with a nervous laugh, "I should warn you, the entire teenage population of our island probably knows you're here by now. Katie's a good worker, but she's got a big mouth. It might not be safe for you to stay here."

He nodded, thoughtful. "Hmm. You could be right. So I guess we should keep one step ahead of them."

Shae looked at him, clearly puzzled. "What do you mean?"

"Invite the girls and a reporter from your local paper to a private party you'll be throwing at the inn."

"Huh?"

"Maybe if we give them what they want, they won't look for it and in turn will leave me alone."

Shae snorted. "I doubt that'll work."

"Why not?"

She slowly shook her head. "You really have no idea how popular you are to those girls, do you? They idolize you. My own sister has been walking around in a trance ever since you got here."

Keith winced at the word "idolize" but mulled over Shae's warning. Yet this was a small coastal town, a lot like his childhood home, and not a large metropolis. He knew it could work, if given the chance. Tiffany wasn't all that bad. Three or four more like her he could handle. Freddie was the only problem, but Keith could take care of him. Spending a few hours with the girls, along with the promise of backstage concert tickets—if they allowed him a few weeks of breathing space and privacy. The lure was too great.

"I think they act that way only because they see me onstage under bright lights, or my face bigger than life, smiling down at them from posters," he explained. "When they see I'm just a normal person, like they are, and we all have a nice visit— maybe even lunch, sandwiches or something—they'll relax and might not look at me like star material. Deep down, they're just a bunch of friendly girls looking for acceptance from someone in the adult world."

"I'm not sure I think them normal, or you either, if you believe that tripe you just dished out. And Freddie is worried about me?" Shae gave a short laugh, though she didn't sound amused. "I suppose I'll need to take out extra insurance— and maybe you should, too—if you're serious about doing this. The seasonal hurricanes we have would be a mild problem compared to the explosive whirlwind that's sure to hit the inn."

His finger lifted and gently traced the line in her forehead. Her eyes widened at his touch. "You worry too much, Shae. Trust me—it'll work out. I have a feeling about this. Now, go tell your sister to invite her friends over after school, and I'll contact the paper."

"A feeling, huh?" Her words came out hoarse. "Tell me, are you on medication? Does your therapist know you've escaped?"

"I'll send him an invitation too." Keith winked and stood. "Let's synchronize our watches for four o'clock. Until then, Comrade." He gave her a mock salute and headed back inside, ignoring her skeptical stare.

three

"Don't open that door! They're like a pack of wild animals—just look what they did to my clothes!"

"Didn't you have a nice visit?" Shae couldn't resist asking.

"You were out there—you saw! I never got a chance to open my mouth and say 'hi.' As soon as they saw me they tackled me!"

"I'm sure they were just trying to be friendly. Let's see, how did you put it? Oh, yes, I remember. They're probably just 'looking for acceptance from someone in the adult world.' "

Keith groaned. "I thought you didn't like to tease."

"Oh, but I'm having too much fun! Shall I serve the sandwiches now?" she asked innocently, eyes wide.

"Okay, Shae. You win. I was wrong—dead wrong." He reached down and plucked off a button that hung by a thread from a shirt he'd purchased only that morning.

Shae's mouth thinned as she watched Keith's actions. "Maybe not. Someone needs to set them straight. Actually, it might work after all." She turned, her hand going to the knob and rotating the lock.

"No! Don't open that door!"

She looked over her shoulder into his panicked eyes. "Trust me, Comrade," she said, echoing his words of yesterday. "They're just a bunch of friendly girls, remember?"

She slipped out of the small, closet-like room they used for personal storage and into the family parlor, firmly closing the door behind her. Before it connected with the jamb, she thought she heard him groan again. She did hear the click of the lock as it was shot back into position.

Looking at the sea of expectant faces, she straightened her shoulders. Friendly girls—ha! What on earth could she say to this wild-eyed throng of fourteen teenagers? How could they have known Tiffany would invite every girl in her class, and not just the three or four expected? It had been a miracle that Shae, Katie, and Gretta had been able to wrest Keith from their clutches.

"Where is he, Miss Stevens?"

"We want Keith Travers," a bold young brunette with braces on her teeth demanded. "Bring him out here!"

"Yeah, Shae. What's the big deal? Are you trying to keep him all to yourself?"

Shae looked in the direction of the voice until she spotted the redheaded culprit. "Liz, I'm surprised at you. At all of you! Most of you come from good homes and were raised better than the wild animals I saw a few minutes ago. What got into you?"

"But that's Keith Travers!" Tamela, a pretty blond with multiple ear piercings, chimed in. There was a stir of agreement, and others begged to see him.

"Yes, that's Keith Travers. And yes, he's been given a talent that must be remarkable, judging from your interest in him. But it doesn't change the fact that he's a person—just like you or me."

Some of the girls looked at one another, evidently not sure what to say in the face of such logic.

"But, Shae, that's dumb."

Trust her sister to argue. Shae ignored Tiffany and continued her speech. "Most of you know what the Bible says about worshipping idols. Right? Well that's what you're doing to Mr. Travers. You're worshipping him as a god—but he's only a man."

"But he's *sooo* good-looking!" A short girl with glitter on her face and neon pink streaks in her hair intoned.

Shae held back a smile at the teen's impassioned words. "Yes, he is. But so is Trent Harmon, the druggist's son—at least that's what some of you have told me. . .and Will Blakely who works on the docks. Yet I'll bet you don't tackle them when they come see you."

"But, Shae, they're ordinary people. Keith Travers is, well— Keith Travers!" a plump girl with freckles jumped in.

"Who is a person—created by God—like Trent and William. And he deserves the same kind of respect you give your friends. You girls put too much value on looks. It's what's inside that counts."

"Aw, my mom says the same thing."

"Well, she's right, Jill."

"It doesn't matter. Keith's still got it all!" the girl with the glittery face exclaimed.

"Admiration is one thing," Shae said patiently. "But idolatry is just plain wrong, as I'm sure you know if you've read your Bibles. Think what happened to the people in the Old Testament who worshipped other gods. Would you want something like that to happen to you? God is serious when He tells us not to do something that's wrong." Shae's last sentences trembled as a flicker of the past returned, and her mother's voice faintly echoed those same words in her mind.

"Aw, Shae, lighten up," Tiffany said, rolling her eyes. "We were just having a little fun."

Shae studied her sister. At least she hadn't been one of those who'd mobbed Keith. " 'Fun'?" she challenged. "If you went to a party, and once you walked in the room you were attacked by a group of people—would you want to stay? Or let's say you were the host, as Keith was, and your guests turned on you the moment they walked through the door. Would you consider that 'fun'? Would you have them over again?"

She watched in relief as her quiet words started to get through to the throng. Several of the girls glanced at each other, uncertain. Some looked down, shame written on their faces.

"We're sorry, Shae," Liz mumbled. "Please tell Mr. Travers we apologize."

A click sounded behind Shae, and she glanced over her

shoulder. Keith opened the door a crack, sticking his head out. "Did I hear my name mentioned?"

Fourteen faces turned to him, most with stars still in their eyes—but no one moved a muscle. With wary steps, he went to stand beside Shae. Fourteen pairs of eyes looked in shock at the demolished shirt he wore over his turtleneck. Most of the buttons were ripped away, the collar torn half off, and a slit parted the side halfway to the armpit.

"Did you want to say something, Liz?" Shae prompted.

The girl with braces elbowed Liz in the ribs. "Ow! All right, just don't do that again, Tracey," Liz whispered loudly in warning. She faced Keith's expectant gaze, turned fiery red and just stared.

"Aw, man. What Liz is trying to say is we're really sorry, Mr. Travers," Tracey said. "We didn't mean to jump on you or tear your clothes, and we promise we won't do it again."

"Yes—please stay!" the others joined in. "We're really sorry. Please stay!"

The clamor of the girls' cries covered Keith's low voice as he spoke into Shae's ear. "Since you won't be my backup singer, remind me to ask Freddie to offer you a job as my bodyguard. You were wonderful."

A tingle crept up Shae's spine at his words and the brush of his warm breath against her skin. Keith turned to the girls and gave them one of his famous smiles.

"How about some sandwiches?"

A medley of agreement and relieved laughter trickled through the room, and Gretta suddenly appeared with a tray of club sandwiches and chips. Even the reporter, who sat in a far corner of the room, smiled and mopped his forehead with a handkerchief.

Looking worried, Keith jerked his head sideways, motioning to the middle-aged man. "What about him?" he murmured to Shae. "Think he'll expound on this episode? And will he wait to release the story until after I return to California, like I asked? Somehow I don't think free concert tickets will buy his silence."

"I don't think you'll have any problem where Mr. Franklin is concerned."

"How can you be so sure?"

Shae smiled secretly. "The ringleader, Tracey—the tall brunette with the braces who tackled you—is his daughter. I imagine he'll be very cooperative under the circumstances."

Keith's smile matched her own. Tiffany shyly walked up to him, her guitar in hand. "Will you sing for us, Mr. Travers? My sister's never heard you sing, and we'd all love it if you would."

A loud chorus of agreement filled the room. Keith turned to Shae in surprise. "You've never heard me sing?"

Shae's face grew hot as all eyes turned her way, and she gave her sister a narrowed look. *Thanks a lot, Tiff.*

"Oh, don't take it personally," Tiffany quickly inserted. "She prefers slower music—like gospel stuff—and says she's too old for the 'bubblegum rock' we listen to. Besides, she's not thrilled with what she calls our 'worldly music' anyway."

If the floor had opened up and swallowed her, Shae would have been greatly relieved. But it stubbornly remained fixed and solid beneath her feet and she still stood next to Keith. Amusement danced in his eyes as he watched her.

"Oh! I didn't mean that the way it sounded. What I meant to say was—"

"I think you've said plenty, Tiffany," Shae interrupted.

Keith tilted his head, as if in thought, then faced Shae's sister. "I'll sing—but I'd like to sing something different than what you're used to hearing from me."

"Uh, okay—I guess." Tiffany shrugged.

Keith strode to the baby grand in the opposite corner of the room and perched on the edge of the glossy bench. Interlacing his fingers, he flexed them to loosen them.

"I didn't know you played piano," Tiffany said, surprised.

He looked at her, then his eyes cut to Shae. "There's probably a lot about me you don't know."

Shae's stomach flipped at his words, which seemed directed only to her. His gaze remained fixed on her a moment longer, then he lowered it to the keyboard and positioned his hands on the yellowed keys. His fingers began to float over the ivories in a familiar tune. Stunned, Shae listened as he sang what had been her grandmother's favorite hymn, "The Old Rugged Cross."

The music reached deep into her soul, as though trying to pull away the cobwebs there and let the light infiltrate what had become a dark tomb. Hot tears sprang to her eyes, and she hastily wiped them away. Goose bumps popped out on her arms at the haunting timbre of his voice. After the final note died, a surrealistic hush settled over the room.

"Wow, that was really great, Mr. Travers. I've never heard you sing like that before."

Tiffany's awed remark punctured the quiet atmosphere as successfully as a needle pricking a latex balloon, and everyone began to talk at once. Even the reporter snapped out of his trance and busily began writing in his notepad.

"Will you sing another one?"

"Sing 'Your Love Alone'—it's my favorite," someone piped up.

Pivoting around on the bench, Keith reached for the guitar. The rest of the hour he spent granting requests, giving a private mini-concert. Shae smiled, looking on. The songs were a little immature for her taste, but the girls seemed to like them. Yet nothing compared with his rendition of "The Old Rugged Cross."

After the sandwiches and chips had been consumed, someone suggested hot buttered popcorn, which Gretta hastened to make. The girls sat cross-legged on the floor around Keith, listening to his stories, laughing at his jokes, and obviously having one of the best times of their young lives.

When it was time to go, they did so reluctantly, saying shy good-byes and promising they would grant him the rest and privacy he needed for the remainder of his stay. Shae had a feeling they would have done so even without the promise of free concert tickets and backstage passes. She knew they'd come to the inn that afternoon expecting to see an idol, but left having gained a friend. Keith Travers was really a pretty amazing guy—much different from the egotist Shae had expected.

✿

Keith let out a relieved breath, plopping onto the sofa. "That went well."

"Hmm, yes." Shae eyed the disorganized room, her lips twisting in a grimace. "I suppose I shouldn't leave this mess for Millie."

"I'll help," Tiffany volunteered, though very halfheartedly.

"No. You have a science report to finish. It's due tomorrow, remember."

"Thanks for reminding me!" Tiffany shot up from her place on the couch. "I better go start writing it."

"Tiffany Lauren Stevens! Do you mean to tell me you haven't even started yet?" Shae exclaimed.

But Tiffany had already darted out the door. Shae turned to Keith. "I don't know what I'm going to do with that girl."

He straightened from picking a few kernels of popcorn off the floor and tossed them on the coffee table. "I wouldn't worry about it. I remember burning the midnight oil, trying to get a report finished that should have been done over a period of days, yet was accomplished in a few hours."

"Yeah, thanks. You're a lot of help," Shae remarked wryly while collecting empty paper cups, plates, and bowls and stacking them. "I can imagine what kind of grades you must've made."

Remembering, he grimaced. "Let's just say they weren't always in the first three letters of the alphabet."

Shaking her head, she threw the party ware into a large rubber trash can Gretta had brought in, and sat on the couch beside him to retrieve a few empty cups that had found their way under the coffee table. "By the way, where was Freddie today? I was surprised he didn't show for the party."

"I didn't think he'd agree with the idea, so I sent him to

collect our luggage at the airport in Providence. He should be returning soon."

She straightened, bunching her brows in puzzlement. "Just who's the boss—him or you?"

"Ours is a very strange working relationship."

"Obviously."

Her gaze went to the ceiling, her mind clearly going on another track. "Three years ago when I became Tiffany's guardian, I never thought it would be so hard to take care of her. Boy, was I wrong."

In rapid succession, Keith tossed four wadded yellow napkins into the trash bin, sinking every one of them. "You've taken on a big responsibility for one so young. How old are you anyway? Twenty-four?"

She wrinkled her nose at him. "Actually I'm twenty-two. So tell me, Keith, did you major in basketball in high school? Is that how you passed senior year?" She motioned to the garbage can across the room.

He grinned. "You found me out. But seriously, Shae, you can't be only twenty-two. You're kidding, right?"

"I don't know if I should be offended by that remark or not. A woman likes to be told she looks younger than her age— unless of course, she's under the age of eighteen," she joked.

"But that means you were only nineteen when you became Tiffany's guardian! Fess up—you're pulling my leg."

"No, I was twenty. I have a birthday coming up." She leaned forward to sweep the popcorn kernels he'd thrown onto the table into an empty bowl. "So, Keith, besides being a famous high school basketball star, as well as a singer and musician, what other secrets does your life hold?"

"I'm beginning to wonder the same about you."

She looked up, startled. "What do you mean?

"You don't like to talk about yourself, and I'm curious as to why. Most of the women I know love the subject."

She gave an airy wave of her hand. "There's nothing too spectacular about me." Her voice had a false ring to it.

"I wouldn't be so sure about that," he drawled. When she didn't respond, he shrugged. "Okay. Mind if I ask some questions?"

"Tiffany told me she sent in my personal history for the contest. Read that—I'm sure it tells all about me."

He smiled. "Well, I'm relieved to know it was your history and not Samantha's. We share a lot of the same hobbies. But the form just glossed over the basics. It didn't get into the real nitty-gritty. Besides, it's much more interesting to talk to a person face-to-face than to read a piece of paper about them. Don't you agree?"

She shrugged, her eyes darting to the doorway.

"First question. How did you come to own this inn?"

She visibly relaxed and set down the bowl. "It belonged to my grandmother. She left it to Tiffany, me, and my brother, Tommy, who's younger than me by seven months. Tommy was born prematurely but evidently thinks he's older, considering the bossy way he treats me sometimes." A sparkle lit her eyes. "I don't mind too much, though, since he lives in Connecticut. He's what you'd call a silent partner. And Tiff won't be able to make any decisions concerning the inn until she's older."

"So your parents are deceased?"

"Yes." The word came out faint, clipped.

"Sorry about that." Keith decided to switch to a lighter topic before he lost her. "Okay. Next question. Did you mean what you said to the girls, when you told them you thought I was good-looking?"

The tense expression left her face and she laughed. "Oh, come on. Don't tell me the famous Keith Travers needs his ego stroked?"

"Just answer the question."

"I find you easy to look at," she admitted with an impish grin.

"Good. I'm glad to hear it."

"Why?"

"Huh-uh. I'm asking the questions, remember?"

She rolled her eyes. "I'm not sure I like this game anymore."

Might as well go for the gold. "Why don't you like to discuss your talent?"

Shae's features sobered into a mask of caution. "I don't know what you mean." She plucked at the bottom of her long satin shirt.

"Why do you run away when someone brings up your singing?"

"Now I know I don't like this game anymore." She tried to rise, but he grasped her arm.

"Please, Shae, just listen a minute." His words came quietly. "I think you would be a great asset to the band, and I wish you'd give it some serious thought. I have a feeling there's more behind your refusal than what you're telling me—and I'd really like to understand. Maybe we could even come up with a solution. Is it because of the travel and the time you would have to spend away from here and your sister? Or does it have something to do with your parents and grandmother? Would they have not approved?"

Her eyes grew panicked. "Leave it be, Keith," she said, her words raspy as she broke loose from his light grip.

Alarmed and a bit stunned by her reaction, he shook his head. "What? What did I say? I don't understand."

"Look, I don't want to talk about it. So please, just drop the subject. Okay?" Tears glistened in her eyes as she clumsily stood. Little black pools appeared underneath her lashes, and she hastily wiped them away with a curled forefinger.

Feeling like pond scum, though he wasn't exactly sure what he'd done wrong, Keith shook his head. "Shae, whatever I said to upset you—I'm sorry."

"Forget it. It's okay, and I'd rather not talk about it anymore." She plucked a tissue from a box, wiped off her fingers, and blotted underneath her eyes. "I think I'll turn in now. It's been a long day."

"It's not even seven o'clock. You haven't had dinner."

"I'm not hungry. And I feel another migraine coming on. You and Freddie will have to eat without me. Night, Keith."

"Night. . . I wish you'd tell me what's bothering you," he added under his breath, watching her trudge away. Keith shook his head in confusion. He was getting as aggressive as Freddie. What had compelled him to push like that? Settling his neck against the top of the sofa, he stared at the ceiling.

Strike three, Travers. You're out.

≈

Shae darted up the stairs, calling herself ten kinds of a fool for losing it like that in front of Keith. His words had brought up old memories, memories better left forgotten. As if she ever could forget.

Pressing her fingertips to her temples, she made little circles, trying to relieve the tension. The headaches were coming more frequently than they used to. Probably because of all the stress she was under—playing a combination of big sister, mother, and warden to her irrepressible sister—though so far the month-long sentence of being grounded hadn't commenced. Add to that the everyday duties of trying to run an inn while dealing with Robert and Hillary's marital problems, and now unexpectedly boarding a teen idol with a penchant for tossing out personal questions—it was a wonder she wasn't a candidate for a padded cell.

Shae sighed and pushed open her door. The welcome sight of her antique four-poster bed greeted her. Not bothering to undress, she grabbed the nearby bottle of pain reliever tablets off her bedside table. Popping two, she washed them down with a glass of water before lying on the chenille spread.

Keith Travers might be gorgeous, but he was just too pushy for Shae's peace of mind. She would have to watch herself.

≈

Keith woke and dressed in a pair of blue jeans and a chunky ivory sweater. It was good to have his things again. The sun's rays beamed through the pale gray-and-white pinstriped curtains of the old-fashioned room, cheering him. He smiled back at the inn's logo of the smiling Rhode Island rooster on the plastic-wrapped cup in the bathroom. At last he could enjoy much-needed privacy and a quiet vacation. With Shae. Despite his failure with her last night, Keith was optimistic this morning.

After zipping through his daily grooming, he hurried to the kitchen, deciding to forgo the continental breakfast being served in the dining room. Disappointment deflated his bubble when he saw Shae wasn't in the family's dining nook. Tiffany stared at him, her eyes still a little dazed.

"Morning, Mr. Travers."

He managed a smile. "My friends call me Keith, Tiffany."

A pleasantly shocked expression covered her face. Gretta set a full plate and a glass of juice on the table in front of Keith. Thanking her, he began buttering a muffin. "So how'd the science report go?"

Tiffany's face crumpled into a grimace. "Don't even ask. I'll be lucky to pass this semester. I never knew biology could be so hard." She glanced at her neon-colored wristwatch. "Oh, no. I'm late!"

She took a swift gulp of orange juice and jumped up from the table, banging her leg against the edge. The juice in Keith's glass rocked and sloshed over. He grabbed a napkin and sponged up the liquid before it could seep through the crack and onto the floor.

Tiffany's face turned as pink as her fuzzy top. "Oops. Sorry—gotta run." She plucked up her bookbag from a nearby chair.

"Wait!"

She glanced over her shoulder at him, looking uncertain. "Yeah?"

"Is Shae not feeling well? I was hoping to talk to her."

"She already ate. I think she's in the old storage room, dusting. Later!"

Keith stared after her. Dusting a storage room?

Tiffany zipped out the door, narrowly missing Gretta, who

carried a large platter of sausage links to one of the waitresses for the breakfast buffet.

"Oh—*meine Himmel!*" The woman exclaimed as she spun around, platter held high, to avoid the hurtling teenager.

Keith shook his head in amusement, Tiffany's boundless energy reminding him of his young sisters. Sobering at the thought of his family, he grabbed another apple cinnamon muffin and left the table, heading in the direction of what he hoped was "the old storage room."

After going down one wrong hall and finding nothing but a linen closet and two locked doors, he backtracked and ran across Millie, the cleaning lady. At his question, she peered at him oddly over her half glasses, but motioned to a hallway on the right. Thanking her, Keith strode to the other end of the inn. Seeing a door open a crack, he peeked inside.

Shae, wearing a long-sleeved blue flannel shirt and a pair of dirty jeans, had her back to him. She perched atop a step stool, meticulously dusting a shelf of breakables with a feather duster. Again her hair was pinned up and covered by the blue bandanna she'd worn the first day he'd come to the inn.

The curtains in the room were drawn, the only light coming from a small fixture in the ceiling. The entire back wall was bracketed with wooden shelves. On each one sat delicate figurines of ceramic, crystal, and porcelain. He walked closer, the wide scatter rug muffling his steps.

"I thought the old saying famous for hired help was 'I don't do windows.' How come Millie isn't doing that?"

Shae jerked and teetered on the step. Hurriedly Keith reached up, placing a hand on each side of her waist to steady her.

"I. . .I didn't hear you come in." She turned her head and looked at him over her shoulder, her eyes wide behind her glasses.

"Obviously. Sorry I scared you."

"I'm okay."

Not wanting to, but knowing he should, Keith removed his

hands from her sides. She took the three steps down the ladder, clutching the feather duster.

"Did you need to see me about something?" she asked, not looking at him.

"Not really. Hey, this is nice." His gaze had lit on one of the figurines—a crystalline angel with golden wings—and he reached toward it, intending to examine it closer.

"Don't touch that!"

Her sharp command stilled his arm. Shocked, he studied her. "Sorry—I only wanted to get a look at the bottom and see the markings. It looks like a collector's piece."

"Yes. . .yes it is. I didn't mean to yell. I'm just a little high-strung today. Had a bad night." Shae nervously ran her fingers through the ostrich feathers of the duster. Dust motes filled the air and she sneezed.

"Bless you," he said, not sure what to say next. Why did she always make him feel like a gawky kid? "You have some nice pieces. Are those Hummels? My aunt collects them too."

"Yes. They were my mother's."

The dead tone of her voice made him wonder, but he'd already decided he wouldn't put her through another episode like last night. Uneasy, he fished for something to say. Spotting a telephone on a white painted desk in a corner of the room reminded him he had business to take care of. "Any chance I can use the phone? I need to make a local call."

"Of course. But doesn't the one in your room work?" she asked, all business again.

"Uh, to tell the truth, I never checked."

"Oh." Shae studied him, her brow lifted curiously, then shrugged. "Sure, you're welcome to use that phone. I'll wait outside." She moved toward the door.

"You don't have to go, Shae," he said hurriedly, not wanting her to leave. "It's no big deal. I only felt that since I'm in the area, I should at least call Mom and say hi."

Shae turned and stared. A frown tilted her mouth downward, and Keith wondered what he'd done wrong now.

"Did you say it was a local call?" she asked.

"Yeah. At least I'm pretty sure it is. She lives on the mainland. If it's not, I'll reimburse you."

She crossed her arms. "Do you mean to tell me, Keith Travers, that you've been here three whole days and haven't contacted your mom, who actually lives in the area? And you're planning to visit her with a *phone call?*"

Keith frowned. "My parents and I didn't exactly part on good terms. They were dead set against me pursuing a singing career."

Her mouth fell open. "You mean you haven't talked to them in four years?"

"I send them a postcard now and then."

"And I'll bet they're just thrilled! After all, a postcard does so much to take the place of actually being there."

Keith's mouth thinned. "Look, Shae, what's it to you? I don't get why you're so concerned whether I see my parents or not."

Sadness washed across her face, making Keith wish he could retrieve his curt words. "I've found you don't really appreciate them 'til they're gone, Keith," she whispered, her eyes filled with pain. "Once that happens, the time for togetherness and for words never spoken—that should have been said—is gone too. And you can never get it back."

"Shae—"

"Don't let that happen, Keith. No misunderstanding is worth it." She hurried past him and out the door.

Keith watched her go, feeling as though a lead weight had dropped on him. Turning his attention to the phone, he picked up the receiver and stopped. He couldn't talk to his mom now. Shae's words bore down hard on his conscience, making him feel like a lowlife. He thought about some of the decisions he'd made these past four years and grimaced. Maybe he was.

Upset, he let the receiver fall back into its cradle with a loud clunk.

four

Shae went over the day's correspondence, pulling her brows together in a frown. Sighing, she wrote a check for the electric bill and put it with the envelopes addressed to the meat and fish markets. Thanks to their parents, she and Tiffany were well-off. There was enough to cover their needs, with a substantial part put away for Tiffany to go to college. Yet if prices continued to escalate, Shae might have to increase room rates, and she didn't want to do that.

She laid the pen down and leaned back in her chair. Closing her eyes, she put her fingers to her temple and tried to massage away the tension. The tension that had taken root since Tiffany had informed Shae that she was a contest winner five days ago.

"You look like you could use a break."

Her eyes flew open and lit upon Keith. He stood in the entrance. "Hope you don't mind—the door was open," he said, motioning to it. "I came to ask if you'd like to take a walk with me. You look as if you could use a breather, and even innkeepers take lunch breaks, right?"

Shae's gaze flew to the antique wooden clock on the wall. Already past noon! Where had the day gone?

Keith pulled a wrapped sandwich from his coat pocket. "I'll even provide lunch," he said with a contagious grin.

Shae arched a brow. "From what I've seen of your eating habits the past several days, you give new meaning to the term 'eating on the run.' "

"When you have to keep up with Freddie, it's the only way to survive. Well, how about it? Consider it a peace offering."

Shae hesitated. She was hungry, and the fresh air might do her head some good. "Just let me get my jacket." On second thought, she took off her glasses, slid them into the upright

45

brass holder, then turned to retrieve her windbreaker.

Outside, they strolled down a winding bicycle path cut through the trees, about a hundred feet from the ocean. Above the wind rustling the branches, she could hear waves gently break on the beach. Dark green shrubs—bayberry and others—dotted the unspoiled beauty of the island. The fresh, salty air was just what Shae needed to clear her head, and she inhaled deeply.

Keith regaled her with entertaining stories of his youth and, after awhile, Shae relaxed, even taking part in the easy conversation. After one particular comment, she halted on the trail and gaped at him, fighting back a smile.

"What's so funny?" He looked at her with pretended offense.

"You can't be serious. You don't actually expect me to believe you took home economics in high school, do you?" She shook her head. "I just can't picture the star player dribbling a basketball while wearing an apron—though it would make an interesting photo for your fan club." She chuckled.

"Ha ha. Very funny." His brows drew together. "What's so strange about my learning to cook? There are world famous gourmet chefs who are men, you know."

"Ah, I see." She nodded like a wise sage. "Then a possible career in the culinary department was your only reason at the time?"

He broke away from her gaze, looking a bit sheepish. "Well, no. I was told by a guy during registration that it was an easy credit and a great way to meet girls."

"Yes, I can believe that," she countered dryly. "But surely the great Keith Travers didn't have problems communicating with the opposite sex?"

"Hey, I had feelings of insecurity too. It was my first year at a new school—I didn't know anyone yet."

"Hmm, maybe," Shae said with a thoughtful tilt of her head. They began strolling again. "Somehow, though, I'd pictured you as the type to escort the homecoming queen to the prom."

She darted him a glance and noticed his reddening face. She laughed. "You did—didn't you?"

"Well, yeah. But only because the captain of the football team—who was a good friend of mine as well as being her boyfriend—ended up in the hospital with a broken hip," he explained hurriedly. "I was the only one he could trust with her, since I had a steady of my own. I took them both."

Shae smiled sweetly, fully enjoying her game. "And were you also on the football team, Keith?"

A pause. "Yeah."

"Top ten?"

He nodded, beginning to look uncomfortable again.

"Aha!" She said, lifting her index finger like a scientist who'd just made a startling new discovery. "Now let's see, the way the popularity cliques work. . .hmm. . .my guess is your girl was on the cheerleading squad. Right?"

He rolled his eyes. "She was the captain."

Shae burst into gales of laughter. "Oh, yeah, Keith. I can see why you were so insecure."

He shook his head with a defeated grin. "Okay, Miss Smarty," he said when she'd quieted down and they resumed their walk, "now it's your turn. You don't look like you were a wallflower. My guess is you were on the drill team, and. . .in your senior year you were voted 'most likely to succeed.' Did I hit the mark?"

Shae swung her startled gaze to him. "Not about my being on the drill team. I was in the choral department for two years."

"Doesn't surprise me a bit. And I'll bet you usually had the lead in the school's musicals."

She flushed and looked away, which answered his remark. "And the other—about being voted most likely to succeed?"

"Yes," she said quickly. "But they were wrong. I wouldn't call being an innkeeper a huge success."

"Maybe not. But I don't think that's where your destiny really lies, Shae."

"Oh, look! Did you see that? I think it's a marsh hawk.

They're endangered, you know."

Keith looked to where she pointed, but could see no evidence of the bird in question.

"So even your school years are off-limits, huh?" he muttered, half to himself.

She bristled. "I don't know what you're talking about."

"I thought you needed glasses to see. Are you sure it was a hawk and not a tree branch? Maybe it broke and fell, or the wind was tossing it around."

"That's silly. Branches don't look anything like birds. Besides, branches don't fly through the air. My vision may be blurry, but I'm not blind."

Without thought, Keith stopped walking and turned, lowering his face until it was inches from hers. The darks of her eyes widened to the size of the cocoa-colored marbles he'd had as a kid.

"And do you see me as a blur, Shae?" he whispered in a low voice. "Can you see me clearly when I get close like this?"

"I. . .I see you okay."

He watched as she caught her lower lip between her teeth. Hurriedly he straightened, wondering what had prompted him to pull such a crazy stunt. He was the one acting like a deranged psychopath, and the last thing he wanted was to startle her away. Yet when he was around her, he couldn't seem to think clearly. *Chill, Travers.*

"Hungry?" he asked with forced lightness. "Let's eat the sandwiches on the way back."

Shae gave a brief nod, and he retrieved two squares wrapped in wax paper from his pocket, handing one to her. Her hands shook a bit as she unwrapped the sandwich. She took a small bite, pulled it away and looked at the bread, puzzled. "Peanut butter and jelly? I thought Gretta was against such plain fare."

"I made them."

"You?"

"There's something about a peanut butter and jelly sandwich that takes a person back to his childhood," he explained.

The glint of mischief was back in her eyes. "Well, I guess I shouldn't be too surprised, being as you took home economics, I mean. Your teacher taught you well, Keith. This is delicious." She took another bite as if to prove her remark.

"You really don't believe I took the course, do you? Took it and passed with flying colors, I might add—though it wasn't as easy as Jim told me it would be."

"Of course I believe you, Keith. Why would you lie?" Her voice danced with merriment.

"All right, Miss Know-it-all, I'll prove it to you. If Gretta will allow me to invade her domain one night, I'll make you a gourmet meal you'll never forget. And never again will you think to doubt the word of Keith Travers."

"You're on. But be warned—I intend to hold you to it. A night of grilled cheese sandwiches and soup might be nice for a change."

"Ha, ha—very funny. You'll see. I'll make you eat those words, Shae Stevens."

"Oh, but I'm sure they couldn't compare to your cooking talents, Keith. I'll just stick to food, thanks."

"I think what you need is a good spanking." He narrowed his eyes and steadily approached her. Giving a laughing yelp of protest, she dodged away and took off down the path. Keith gave chase. After letting her take the lead for a short time, he closed in and grabbed her arm. She squealed but didn't try to break away when he pulled her around to face him.

Out of breath, they stared at one another. Shae's face was rosy from running, and her eyes sparkled with a life of their own. Perspiration dotted her upper lip.

"You have jelly on the corner of your mouth," he panted, his voice low.

The tip of her tongue flicked to the purple spot, licking it away. His eyes stayed riveted to her mouth. He had never wanted to kiss anyone so badly. Forcing himself to look away, Keith pushed a shaky hand through his hair, sweeping it off his forehead. "I think we'd better head back."

Needing to touch her, he allowed himself to reach for her hand and was thankful she didn't pull away. They didn't speak a word the entire walk back. When they reached the side of the inn, Keith stopped, Shae's hand still enfolded in his.

She looked at him, questions in her eyes.

Unable to help himself, he lifted her hand to his lips and kissed the tips of her curled fingers lightly. He loved watching her eyes soften in wonder.

"I'd better let you get back to work now. I know you're busy." A movement from a top window caught his eye, and he looked up to see a curtain flutter into place.

Shae followed his gaze. The dazed expression left her features, and her mouth drew into a grim line. "Tiffany's room," she muttered. "I'll talk to you later, Keith. I have some business to attend to."

Reluctantly, he let go of her hand and watched her march to the front of the inn.

❧

Shae knocked on her sister's door, then pushed it open without waiting for an answer. Tiffany lay on her back on the twin bed, her arms underneath the pillow. Her gaze was fastened to the ceiling, and a big smile spread over her face. The flowered curtain at the window was cracked slightly.

Shae approached the foot of the bed and crossed her arms. "Why aren't you in school, Tiff?"

"It's spring break."

"Oh," Shae muttered with a defeated breath. "I'd forgotten that was coming up."

Tiffany jumped up to a kneeling position and clutched her pillow, her eyes dancing. "He kissed your hand!" She threw the pillow in the air and caught it with a delighted little laugh.

Memory of Keith's lips on her skin made Shae tingle all over again. She forced herself to stay mad and address the issue at hand. "So, you *were* spying!"

"Hey, it's not a crime to look out your own window." Tiffany shrugged. "Besides I'm grounded, remember?"

For the first time Shae wished she could revoke the month-long sentence.

"Anyway, Liz was right—she said it would happen, but I didn't believe it. Wait 'til I tell her! It'll cost me my new CD, but it's worth it."

Shae gritted her teeth. "That's the second time you've mentioned Liz being right concerning my situation with Keith. I want to know what you're talking about, and I want to know this minute."

Tiffany shrugged. "Okay. I guess I can tell you now. When Keith came back to the inn, Liz said she'd bet the bad weather wasn't the only thing that brought him back. After we found out we—I mean you—had won the contest, Liz had a feeling that when Keith met you, he'd take you out anyway, and might even fall for you even if you weren't Samantha. I wasn't sure after your first meeting. I mean, face it, Shae, you weren't looking your best."

"Thanks for the compliment."

"Awww, Shae. You know what I mean. You were all dirty from cleaning and had that awful plaid shirt on—and your hair hidden by that bandanna you wear, and not one speck of makeup on, and those dumb glasses—"

"If you keep it up, little sister, you'll turn my head with your flattery."

Tiffany grinned. "You're really a knockout when you try. But until Keith came into the picture you just haven't cared much about trying."

"Oh, I don't know. . . ."

"I'm not talking about when you play hostess. I'm talking about just any old day. Look at you—I think that's the first time I've seen you wear a pretty ribbon in your hair instead of pulling it back with just a rubber band. And you're wearing lipstick too!"

Shae blushed, but stood her ground. "I often wear something on my lips."

"Lip balm doesn't count. Hey, don't get so defensive—I

think it's great. It's about time you had something to attract you—like a man in your life. And Keith Travers definitely fits that bill!"

"Why, Tiff? Why the sudden interest in my social calendar?"

"But that's just it! You don't have a social calendar. Besides working at the inn, you're life is just one big zero. Soon—if I ever pass biology that is—I'll be off to college and start a career and maybe even get married. And what will you do, Shae? Just puddle around The Roosting Place until you get old like Grandma? At least she had a life first."

"That's piddle, not puddle."

Tiffany rolled her eyes. "Whatever."

"I appreciate your concern for my welfare, little sister, but I assure you there's no need."

"I know. Like I said—Liz was right."

"Oh—you're impossible!"

Exasperated, Shae turned to leave. Keith's handsome face smiled down at her from a poster, bigger than life. She felt herself turn an embarrassed red, as if he'd actually heard their conversation. Ridiculous! Averting her eyes, she left the room.

❧

"There you are. What're you watching?"

Keith entered the dark private family parlor where Shae sat on the sofa in front of the TV, her legs drawn up beneath her while she munched on a bowl of popcorn. "A movie on the life of Jesus."

"Sounds good. Okay if I join you?"

Her heart gave a nervous little lurch, but she nodded. He sank to the cushion beside her while reaching into her small bowl for a large handful of popcorn.

"Help yourself," she said dryly.

"Thanks. I will."

"There's more in the kitchen if you'd like your own bowl."

"No thanks, I'll just eat out of yours." He threw a few kernels into his mouth. "Hmm. Needs more salt. More butter wouldn't hurt either."

"Right. I forgot you were a connoisseur of foods."

He threw her a grin. "By the way, I talked to Gretta. Tomorrow night plan for the meal of your life—say at seven? I guarantee, you won't forget it."

"That reminds me, I need to write antacid on the grocery list." She gave him an impish smile.

"You just don't quit, do you? Well, you'll see. Meanwhile, I'm going to the kitchen and doctor this popcorn." He stood and reached for her bowl, which she firmly held.

"No thanks. I like it this way."

"That's because your taste buds have grown used to it. Wait until you taste mine." He jerked the bowl out of her hands with a firm tug and strode out the door.

Shae blew a stray wisp of hair from her temple. She was hungry, and now he'd taken her popcorn—some nerve! Still, he did have an endearing boyish quality about him.

Soon Keith returned, triumphantly bearing a huge bowl of buttery popcorn that smelled delicious. Shae smothered the smile that had stuck to her face while she'd been thinking of him—the entire time he'd been gone.

"Wait 'til you taste this!" He sat back down beside her.

"I've heard a starving person will eat anything."

"Just for that, maybe I shouldn't let you have any." He held the bowl out of her reach.

"Ke-eith," she groaned. "I haven't eaten since that sandwich at lunch."

"Apologize."

"Okay, you win. I'm sorry," she muttered, the tantalizing aroma making her mouth water.

He replaced the bowl on his lap and casually looped his arm around her, his hand resting on her shoulder. Large butterflies ran relays in her stomach.

"Did I miss much?" he asked.

"Just commercials." Her voice sounded funny. She ate some of the popcorn so she wouldn't have to talk. It was good. After a few more handfuls, she glanced his way. "How did you manage to make the butter stick to each kernel?"

"Do you like it?" he asked, grinning.

"I have to admit, this is some of the best popcorn I've eaten. When I make it, not all the popcorn gets buttered—even when I shake the bowl. So, how did you do it?"

"Trade secret." He winked.

"Kee-eith!"

"Shh. The movie's starting."

Determined to discover his secret later, Shae watched the opening credits of the historical drama and contentedly munched her popcorn. Gretta came in with two soft drinks and set them down on the coffee table. Shae thanked her and invited her to watch, but she declined with a smile and quickly left. Strange. Gretta loved movies based on Christ's life.

Shrugging to herself, Shae settled against the cushion. She and Keith bantered during commercials, quieting once the movie came back on.

Toward the end, she sniffled when Jesus raised Lazarus from the dead. Tears dripped down her cheeks when He was betrayed and arrested. She cried quietly when they beat Him and nailed Him to the cross. The moisture sped down her cheeks at the end of the movie after He'd risen and the music from the "Hallelujah Chorus" filled the room; she used the sleeve of her sweater to blot the wetness. But when the actor who had the role of Jesus looked lovingly into the camera while the background music reached its crescendo, and said "Lo, I am with you always, even until the end of the world," she really lost it. She buried her face in her hands—and wailed through the entire list of credits.

৵

Keith helplessly looked around the darkened room lit only by the flickering TV. At last seeing the dim outline of what he was searching for, he hurried to a lamp table in the far corner, plucked a couple of tissues from a box, then changed his mind and picked up the whole thing. Returning to Shae's side, he stuck the box in her hand. She thanked him and began to swipe at her eyes with the tissues.

"I–I'm sorry." She hiccupped softly. "Th–this is the second time I've cried around you. But those kinds of m–movies get me every time." She pulled another tissue from the box, dabbed the tears from her cheeks, took a deep breath and gave him a trembling smile. "You must think I'm a silly, hopeless female—and you're right. I probably look like a raccoon by now." She gave a shaky laugh. "I don't know why I don't just quit wearing this stupid mascara."

His heart beginning to hammer, Keith lifted his hand and stroked her glistening cheek with the back of his fingers. "Actually, I think you're pretty wonderful. . .I think you're quite beautiful. . .and I think I'm going to kiss you."

Her eyes widened. Before she could say anything more, Keith lowered his mouth to hers.

A car salesman came on the screen, trying to convince anyone who would listen that he had the best deal in town. Keith shut him out, concentrating only on the woman in his arms. Shae tasted like buttered popcorn, his new favorite flavor. She clung to his shirt as if she were drowning, and he was her life preserver. Keith moved his lips to her cheek then upward to her temple. She exhaled softly, her warm breath fanning his skin. Feeling his pulse race, he lowered his head to reclaim her lips, and she inched her arms up around his neck.

"Hey, what's going on—why's it so dark in here?"

Suddenly they were immersed in a bath of artificial light. Shae pulled away, and Keith shot his gaze toward the door and the intruder. Freddie walked into the room. "Looks like I got here just in time," he drawled, the ever present unlit cigar clamped between his teeth.

Shae jumped up from the couch, red suffusing her face. "I'm going to bed. G'night, Freddie—night, Keith." Before he could say a word, she fled from the room.

"You have all the finesse of a bull in a china shop," Keith muttered.

"What's that supposed to mean?"

"Never mind." Keith sighed and whisked a hand through his hair, brushing it away from his forehead. "What did you want anyway? Couldn't it have waited 'til morning?"

"I didn't intend to intrude on your little love scene. But maybe it's good that I did." Freddie's eyes narrowed. "I'd advise you to stay away from her, Travers. She's a strange bird—"

"Watch it," Keith warned. "Be careful how you talk about Shae."

"Oh, so that's how it is," Freddie grumbled. "Like I said, I'm in favor of you finding a love interest—but not with a woman who might have psychotic tendencies. . . ."

Infuriated, Keith stood and raised both hands upright at his sides at chest level. "I refuse to hash this out again. Our conversation is over. She's not what your deranged mind has dreamed up, but I don't suppose anything will convince you of that. Good night."

Keith stomped up the stairs to his room, tired of Freddie thinking he owned him just because Keith signed a piece of paper years ago. Yet he was just as angry with himself as he was with his manager. He hadn't meant to kiss Shae yet, though he was elated by her warm response to him. But he meant what he told Freddie. She was special, and Keith was determined to treat their budding relationship with care. That is, if he was ever given the chance again.

five

Shae tried to focus on the printed page of the ledger she used for recording reservations, but her eyes felt scratchy. She leaned back in the chair and massaged her closed eyelids with her fingertips. Sleep had eluded her until the wee hours of morning, until she'd at last fallen into exhausted slumber for three hours before her alarm raided disturbing dreams.

"You okay?"

Her eyes flew open at the familiar voice, and her heart tripped. Keith stood in the doorway, dressed to go out. Brown corduroy jeans covered his long legs, and an ivory ribbed turtleneck enhanced the bronzed glow of his skin. Wheat blond hair brushed the collar of his dark brown bomber jacket. The usual pair of designer sunglasses covered his eyes. He looked like he belonged on the cover of an outdoor magazine.

Shae remembered to breathe. "I guess I've just been working too hard. My eyes feel a little tired."

"Where are your glasses?"

"I left them upstairs. Sometimes when I do book work without them, my eyes start to hurt." She shrugged. "It's really no big deal. I'll live."

"Hmm. I think what you need is some fresh air and sunshine. Wanna come with me?"

"Where to?"

He gave her one of his heart-stopping smiles. "I need to pick up some things for tonight's meal. Have you forgotten?"

No. She hadn't forgotten. She hadn't forgotten anything. Just being in his presence was doing crazy things to her insides. And after last night, she didn't think it wise to be alone with him more than was necessary.

How many others had he kissed? Immediately Shae

57

retracted the mental question, deciding she'd rather not know. She didn't need to know. She wouldn't be another conquest, adding herself to the long line of women that must be in his past. Strong values had been instilled in her since childhood, and even for the famous Keith Travers, Shae wouldn't give them up.

"Shae?"

She blinked. *It's just an outing to the store. Not a weekend getaway,* she reminded her foolish brain. "Sure, I'll go with you." She rose from the chair and grabbed her jacket slung over the back.

"By the way, do you have a car?"

"It's only a few blocks to the market, Keith. Walking distance."

"I know, but we're going to the other side of the island."

She quit pushing her arm through the jacket sleeve and stared. "Why?"

"Because the ingredients I'm looking for, the market doesn't have. I called and found them at a larger grocer's though."

"Doesn't have?" She eyed him with suspicion. "What are you looking for, Keith? Cow's tongue? Pig's feet? Snails?"

He grinned. "Actually, they are considered delicacies."

She let out a little moan and continued shrugging into her windbreaker. "I think I'd better get a large box of that antacid."

"Trust me, Shae. I think you'll be pleasantly surprised."

Hoping he was right, but doubting it, she stopped at the front desk for her car keys and led him around the side of the inn to the small, private garage. She tossed him the keys. "You drive—my eyes hurt."

He slipped behind the wheel. Shae got in on the other side and laid her head against the seat. Blissfully, she closed her eyes.

Soon Keith turned onto another road. The sun poured into the passenger side window, ruthlessly attacking her shut eyelids. Shae sat up and groped through the glove compartment, finding a pair of dark sunglasses with one of the temples missing. They hadn't been like that the last time she'd worn them. No doubt Tiffany was responsible for their present condition. But even broken sunglasses were better then none at all. Shae rammed them onto her nose and laid her head back again.

It seemed she'd just fallen asleep when her arm was grasped and she was gently shaken. She mumbled incoherently, pushing Keith's hand away.

"Wake up, Shae. We're here."

At his soft, insistent words, she opened her eyes, but they still felt gritty. "I'm not much company. Maybe I should just stay in the car while you go in," she murmured, tilting her head against the window.

"Actually, I've enjoyed your company. When you snore, it sounds almost musical."

"I do not snore!" His teasing words had the effect of a dousing of icy water. Sitting upright, she turned and glared at him through the crooked dark glasses, daring him to say otherwise.

His lips flickering at the corners as though holding back a smile, he pulled off his sunglasses and concentrated hard on cleaning them with the bottom of his shirt. Finally he looked her way with a hopeful expression. "Come with me, Shae. . . please?"

"Oh, all right," she muttered. How could she resist those gorgeous eyes? She imagined he would probably have a lucrative business selling ice cream to Eskimos, or saunas to the Arabs in the Syrian Desert, if he chose to do so.

Keith put his sunglasses back on and got out of the car. Reluctantly, Shae removed her broken ones, set them on the dashboard, and followed him into the grocery store. She watched as he searched the narrow aisles, selecting various items. As they were heading to the checkout, she gave him a puzzled glance.

"Is this meal vegetarian? You didn't buy any meat or fish."

"Trust me, Shae."

She rolled her eyes in exasperation, tired of hearing those

words. Noticing a box of antacid on the end aisle next to the cash register, she grabbed it and put it with the other items. "For the guests," she said innocently when Keith cast a suspicious glance her way. "I was serious when I said I needed to restock. I'll pay you back."

Keith shrugged it off. "Don't worry about it."

Their turn came up. He pulled an eel-skin wallet out of his back pocket and riffled through it. "I'll have to use a credit card," he told the blond cashier after she'd rung up the items. "I seem to be out of cash."

She barely looked at him or the card as she slid it and the charge slip into the old metal contraption and moved the handle back and forth with a snap. She pulled out the slip, marked on it, then placed it in front of Keith for him to sign, her bored gaze lifting to his.

Blue-violet eyes grew wide, her pink lips parting in a look of disbelief. She stared down at the paper with his signature and gasped. "It *is* you! I can't believe it." Her eyes lifted to his, adoration now written in them. "Will you sign this for me?"

Keith smiled. "I think I already have."

"Oh, not the charge slip," she laughed, pushing it away as if it were of little importance. She pulled a thick pad of paper from her green smock. "This. I'd like your autograph. Address it to Kitty, please. . . . Keith Travers on our little island—I still can't believe it. I waited on Keith Travers! Oh, wait 'til the other girls hear—they'll never believe me. Too bad I don't have a camera. . . ."

Keith hurriedly signed the pad while the cashier rambled on, gushing over him. He began to look uneasy when a couple of curious women shoppers stopped what they were doing to listen to the enamored cashier's words. Even the bag boy moved at a snail's pace, staring at Keith while clumsily sacking the purchases. The bottle of sparkling cider missed the bag and hit the counter with a bang.

"Oh, thank you! Thank you so much!" Kitty clutched the paper to her heart, her hands trembling.

"Uh, can I have my card back now?" Keith asked, his eyes darting around the area.

"Oh, of course. Silly me! Here." She handed him the card. Snatching it out of her hand, he plucked up the sack of groceries.

"Look! It *is* him—it's Keith Travers!" came a squeal from several aisles away.

"Oh, no," Keith groaned. He grabbed Shae's hand, pulling her with him as he sped to the glass door. His shoulder accidentally brushed a teetering display of straw containers stacked by the entrance. Shae winced when she heard muffled thuds as the baskets fell and rolled over the tile floor behind them. Keith didn't stop, but flew through the door—almost running down an elderly gentleman and his wife as they approached the store.

"Oh!" the woman exclaimed, putting a hand to her bosom.

"Sorry!" Keith yelled over his shoulder, not stopping until he reached the car. He yanked open the driver's door, jumped inside, and slammed it shut, Shae following suit on the passenger side. She looked over her shoulder at the store's entrance.

Kitty had run out and was waving a slip of paper above her head. "Wait, you forgot your receipt!" Three teenaged girls ran past, their eyes eagerly scanning the parking area. When they saw Shae's car, they gave a shout and scampered toward it.

"Hold on!" Keith jammed the key into the ignition, started the car, and took off with a squeal of burning rubber as the tires spun on black tarmac. Shae turned on the seat and looked behind her at the three disappointed faces. One of the teens burst into tears when she realized her idol had gotten away.

"Guess I was wrong to trust Tiffany's friends," Keith said in a clipped tone.

"Those three weren't at the party. In fact, I've never seen them before. They must be tourists." When he didn't answer, just gave an abrupt nod, Shae tried for levity, hoping to break the tension. "I'd hate to be the next customer in Kitty's aisle.

There's no telling when she'll come down to earth." When Keith still didn't respond, she queried softly, "Is it always like that?"

"Always," he bit out, then groaned. "Sometimes I can't even go outside my apartment to get the paper without finding one of them camped on my lawn, even though I do live in a high security area. No one can get through the gate without punching in a code," he explained, "but it doesn't seem to do any good. I've moved six times in four years—and they always still seem to find me. I had thought on this small island I wouldn't have that kind of problem, but I guess Freddie is right. I can't go anywhere without the hassle." He hit the steering wheel with the flat of his hand.

Not certain what to say, Shae kept quiet and let him spill.

"Privacy is a luxury I can't even remember," he gritted. "I like what I do—sing and write songs—but sometimes I wonder if it's worth it. You know what I'm saying?" He shot a glance her way, a frown marring his brow.

"Believe me, Keith. I understand better than you realize," she said under her breath, then wished she hadn't.

He let out a frustrated sigh, obviously not hearing her words. "I'm sorry, Shae. I know you weren't feeling good to begin with. Just once, I'd like to go somewhere without being recognized."

"You could always wear a dark wig," she joked.

"Believe me, I've thought about it."

"Maybe you're singing for the wrong audience." The words tumbled out of her mouth before she thought twice.

Keith briefly looked her way, his brows bunched in a puzzled frown. "What do you mean?"

Shae squirmed in her seat. Yes, what did she mean? Memory of the day he'd sung "The Old Rugged Cross" hit her. She remembered, too, the feeling in the atmosphere and the awed faces in the room.

"God gave you a wonderful talent, Keith. Maybe He wants you to use it for Him."

Yeah, you're one to talk, Marcia Shae. Wincing, she tried to block out the sardonic thought. She wouldn't blame Keith if he threw those same words in her face, as many times as he'd tried to convince her to sing.

A nerve near his jaw tensed and there was an uncomfortable pause before he responded. "My granny said the same thing. She was one of the strongest believers I've known."

Shae blinked. He had used the word *believers*—a word used by those of the Christian faith. Did that mean. . .?

Keith glanced sideways and studied her fixed gaze. "Well, aren't you going to ask me?"

"Ask you what?" Shae's mouth felt dry.

"If I'm a Christian. I've seen the look in your eyes when you've prayed at mealtimes. I'm surprised you haven't said anything yet."

"Okay," she whispered. "Are you?"

He gave a self-deprecating laugh. "Well, I walked right into that one." His face sobered, looked sad. "I was. I accepted Jesus as my Savior at a youth camp when I was twelve. But, well, I guess the draw to the limelight was too strong." He sighed and shook his head.

"You don't sound too happy with your life," Shae said, somewhat surprised.

"Could be because I'm not. One day, the limelight doesn't shine so brightly anymore, and you look around and wonder how you got where you did. At least, that's what happened to me." He gave her a sober glance. "I'm twenty-five, Shae. I've achieved in four years what most men dream of in a lifetime—wealth, success, and fame. But still that void is always there, sucking me dry."

Shae squirmed at the turn of conversation. She understood about that void all too well. "So tell me how you got started in the business." She forced a bright tone to her voice, one she didn't feel.

He threw her a puzzled look, a flicker of hurt in his eyes. Shae inwardly cringed, not wanting to seem unfeeling, but she just couldn't talk about voids and God right now.

"When I wasn't playing sports, I spent every spare moment I had in bands all through junior high and high school," he said after awhile. "Music was my first love. I remember writing and singing songs when I was eleven and hoping someday I'd be a musician. I learned guitar and piano when I was a just a squirt—thanks to Mom's influence. The sax, too—though that only lasted two years. I got into school sports because that's what Dad wanted, though I can't say I didn't enjoy playing them."

He shrugged. "After high school, I won a regional music contest and was offered a recording contract. Against my parents' wishes I took it. I'd just turned twenty-one, so there wasn't much they could do to stop me. Star Artists offered me a better contract after that one expired, and here I am. I guess you could say I'm like the modern-day prodigal—only I haven't gone home."

"You still could, you know."

"What?"

"Go home."

Silence.

"Keith, I've been thinking about where I want to go on our date."

"Yeah?" he asked warily.

"I'd like to meet your family." What she really wanted was for him to be reunited with them.

"I don't think that's a good idea, Shae," he said after another span of thick silence. "Remember, someone from the magazine will be there. I don't want to make a three-ring media circus out of what should be a quiet family gathering."

She sighed. "Yeah, I see your point. But I still think you should visit them while you're in Rhode Island—especially since you said they live in the area. Just think how they would feel if they discovered you were here and didn't even bother to visit."

"I'll think about it."

Nothing more was said during the drive back to the inn. Shae studied his grim countenance, wondering if she'd gone too far. How could she get him to realize just how important it was to be part of a family unit with a mother and father who cared? The times of togetherness, the unconditional love, the support that only parents could give their children. . . All these were lost to her now. She supposed the old adage was true that people didn't appreciate what they had until it was gone. How she wished she could turn the hands of time backward and be given a second chance.

Idly, she stared out the window at the pastel-painted summer cottages and renovated historical homes they passed. Her favorite on this street, the gray one with white trim and the crow's nest, didn't even make her smile like it usually did.

When they reached the inn, Keith pulled in front, but didn't turn off the motor. "There's still something I need to take care of," he said, not looking at her.

Shae stepped out and took the stairs to the wraparound porch. She stood at the rail, watching the car disappear down the coastal road. Had she blown it?

≈

Shae studied the contents of her closet, trying to decide what to wear. She hadn't talked to Keith since he'd returned a few hours earlier, but since he hadn't informed her otherwise, she assumed tonight's dinner was still on. Anxiety made her hands shake as she slid a dress along the rod.

The private phone on her bedside table emitted a shrill ring, demanding attention. She thought about ignoring it, then blew out an irritated breath, ran across the room to grab it on the fifth ring, and gave a halfhearted "Hello?"

"How's one of my favorite sisters doing? You're not an easy person to get ahold of. Where were you earlier?"

"Tommy?" Smiling, she sank onto her four-poster bed. "It's good to hear from you. How's Linda?"

"Badgering me about taking a vacation. That's why I called. I thought we might come down next week—say

Wednesday? Think you can spare a room?"

"Of course. You know better than to ask."

"How's Tiffany?"

Shae groaned. "Don't ask."

"Up to her usual tricks, huh?"

"You won't believe the latest."

"Save it 'til I get there, Sis. There's something I need to talk to you about. I'd better go for now, though. Long distance rates are still too high for my tastes. See you next Wednesday!"

"Yeah, bye." Shae replaced the phone, uneasy, then mentally chastised herself. Just because Tommy wanted to discuss something with her didn't necessarily mean it was something negative. But he had sounded so strange. Determined to forget her brother for now, Shae again approached her walk-in closet.

An hour later she studied the person in the mirror, wearing the royal blue silk dress. Who was that girl staring back? She seemed so calm, so confident—nothing like Shae really felt. Turning her back on the illusory image, she went downstairs.

Keith stood waiting on the landing, looking far too handsome in a blue cotton shirt that matched his eyes and a pair of gray slacks. A contemporary tie in swirls of blues hung neatly from his collar. When he caught sight of her, his eyes lit up and glowed with approval. Shae's heart beat a little faster.

"Very nice," he murmured, making her cheeks grow warm. He put a hand to her elbow and steered her toward a room they kept reserved for private parties.

"I thought we were eating in the kitchen or the dining room," she said, hating the nervous warble in her voice.

"Gretta told me about this room, and I thought it would be more appropriate. Relax, Shae, I won't bite."

More appropriate? For what? She followed him into the cozy room, her pulse rate increasing in tempo like a rapidly ticking metronome atop a piano. A linen and lace cloth lay draped over a round table. Two elegant place settings sat across from one another. A short crystal vase with blue and white flowers stood in the center.

Shae remained near the door, uncertain.

Keith had pulled out a chair and now looked at her. "Wouldn't you like to sit down and eat?"

"I wasn't planning on standing." Nervousness put a bite to her words.

A confused vee formed between his brows. "Shae, I don't know what happened in the last few hours to make you look at me like the big bad wolf that's ready to eat you. But let's try to have a nice evening anyway. Okay?"

She knew she was acting silly, but couldn't seem to help it. First dates were scary enough, she'd heard. But when the date was with someone like Keith, who'd taken out so many glamorous, popular women in his lifetime. . . Shae clenched her hands in determination. This wasn't an actual date. She'd eaten with him other times, though usually in the presence of others. The only difference tonight was that they were dressed up and using good china instead of stoneware. And they were alone.

She swallowed and, with what she hoped passed for a normal smile, moved toward him and sat down. "Something smells great."

"That's music to my ears, coming from you," Keith said, taking the chair across from her. To her surprise, he bowed his head and said the blessing for both of them. The words were rusty, as if he hadn't prayed in awhile, but they sounded sincere.

Shae bit the inside of her cheek, knowing she needed to clear the air before they went any further. "Keith, about this afternoon, I'm sorry. I know I wasn't very nice."

He gave her a soft smile. "Forget it. I'm sorry too. Now eat!" he quietly commanded with a boyish smirk.

She couldn't help but grin. His smiles were infectious.

As the meal progressed, his easygoing attitude soon helped relax her. She toyed with a forkful of crab quiche and cocked her brow. "Say, Keith, didn't I hear something once that real men don't eat—"

"Don't say it," he said, rolling his eyes.

She chuckled and popped one of the peppery fried smelts in her mouth. "Hey, this is good."

"You sound surprised," he said in mock indignation. "But don't worry, I won't say I told you so. Even if I did." His smile was smug.

She chose to ignore him and focus on the food.

"Try some of the shrimp paste," he encouraged, handing her a platter with a bowl of dip surrounded by herb crackers.

She took an oval cracker and dipped it into the paste. It was delicious—everything was. Even the garden salad—made with three kinds of lettuce, grated carrots, and bits of green peppers—was a treat to the taste buds. Chocolate mousse followed, creamy and rich. After scraping her dish with her spoon and draining the last drop of sparkling cider from her glass, Shae sat back, giving a contented sigh.

"Well, Keith, when I'm wrong I admit it. Remind me to send a thank-you card to your home economics teacher. Did you really learn all this in high school?"

He nodded. "I've learned a lot since then too. I told myself being a bachelor doesn't mean I'm going to be stuck with a life of frozen dinners and takeouts. You'd be amazed at how easy a cookbook is to follow when you've had the training."

"I guess I took the wrong classes—I should have taken home ec. I can't even boil an egg." She giggled. "I tried once, but the water boiled over, the egg cracked, and all that filmy white stuff inside poked out the middle."

Keith smiled, his expression tender and his eyes full of something Shae didn't understand. Her heart began to race. Quickly she lowered her gaze to her empty dish and stared, feeling her muscles begin to tighten again.

After about a minute of silence, he threw his napkin to the table and stood. "How about a walk by the ocean?"

She thought about her two-inch heels. "I'm not dressed for it."

"Well then, want to check out the floor show?"

"I know it forward and backward."

"Okaaay. Shall we see what's on TV?"

Remembering what happened the last time they'd watched television together, Shae gave a quick shake of her head. "No, thanks. The meal was superb and I thoroughly enjoyed it, but if you'll excuse me, I think I'll turn in early."

"I don't think so."

Her eyes widened at this unexpected response. He crossed his arms over his chest, his stance nonchalant yet almost formidable at the same time.

Her heart skipped a beat. "Excuse me?"

"I don't know why you're suddenly uncomfortable to be in my company, but I intend to find out what's going on in that imagination of yours if it takes all night. Ladies first," he said, motioning to the door.

"Where to?"

"To your family parlor, to discuss this like two mature adults. After you?" Again he gestured to the door with a sweep of his hand.

Shae wondered if Keith would chase her up the stairs if she headed that way. As stubborn as he was, he probably would. She grimaced. With Keith around digging up her buried secrets, she didn't stand a chance. Yet she determined he would *never* uncover her darkest one.

six

Shae preceded Keith into the parlor and sank to the far end of the couch. He watched her move a small beaded throw pillow on the cushion beside her, preventing him from sitting there. Perched on the edge of the sofa, she reminded him of a wary bird poised for flight. Her back was ramrod straight, her hands clasped tightly in her lap, and her eyes had the look of one hunted.

He gave a world-weary sigh. "Shae—"

She raised a hand to stop him. "Allow me to save you the trouble of delving into my inner mind and bringing out all my close-kept secrets. I know for some strange reason you insist on knowing all the answers about me—though I can't begin to understand why—and that you won't stop until you get them.

"So, okay, Keith, here it is. Brace yourself. The terrible truth is I've never dated—not even in high school—and this is the first time I've shared dinner, alone, with a man. So go ahead and laugh. I wouldn't blame you one bit."

"You never dated?" Keith shook his head, flabbergasted. She was so pretty, sweet, and fun to be with, as well as highly intelligent. Were the men on this island blind, stupid, or both?

Shae flicked her long hair over one shoulder in a nervous gesture. "It wasn't that my parents didn't allow it—though they said I had to wait until I was sixteen. It's just that we were so busy. Moving all the time, never really settling down, always on the go. I. . .I didn't always live on the island."

She paused, tightly clasped her hands on her lap, and stared at them. Keith waited patiently, afraid to say anything that might make her clam up again. He took a seat a couple of feet away from her on the couch, respecting her wish for distance.

"Occasionally I would go with a boy and other friends to a

pizza place," she continued. "My parents allowed group dates. But I never got the chance to get to know someone well, because of all the moves. Then after. . .after they died. . .for awhile I just didn't care about anything anymore. Later my grandmother had a stroke and there wasn't time to form any new relationships what with running the inn and taking care of Tiffany and everything else to do. . . ."

"You poor kid." He reached over to lay a hand on her clenched ones, but Shae snatched them away before he could make contact. She shot to her feet and faced him, her chin lifted proudly.

"I didn't tell you this to gain your pity, Keith." Her voice and emotions were in control again. "I just felt I owed you an explanation for my strange behavior tonight. And I am *not* a kid!"

"Bad choice of words, sorry," he muttered. He thought a moment. "That's why I had such a hard time convincing you to go on the contest date with me, isn't it?"

She nodded.

Something else dawned on him. "Why, I'll bet you'd never been kissed before either!"

Her face grew rosier. "A few quick pecks on the lips by a fifteen-year-old boy were all I experienced. Until you came along."

"Then last night. . ."

As if a lightbulb flashed on inside his head, chasing away the darkness of ignorance, Keith suddenly understood. Because of her inexperience, she must think his repeated attempts at getting to know her were a ploy to use her for selfish purposes—ultimately to hurt her in the end. *That's* probably why she'd been so distant. She was afraid to get close.

"Shae, now I have a confession to make. Please, sit down."

Her brow crinkled in an uncertain frown. Slowly, she sank to the cushion beside him and grabbed the pillow, cradling it to her breast, as though it were a shield.

"Contrary to what you've heard or read about me, I haven't

chosen to date anyone for over a year," he said in a low voice. When she would have interrupted, he held up a hand to stop her. "Doubtless you've heard of different women, whom I've been seen with on dates. But my manager arranged all of them for publicity. They were not my own idea."

He averted his gaze, feeling uneasy and a bit ashamed with what he was about to tell her. "When I first got into the business, I was bowled over by instant fame. I let it get to my head and sowed a few wild oats, went a little crazy. But the women I knew were hard, and those kinds of relationships soured fast." He glanced at her. "Shae, the other night when I kissed you—"

Her face reddened, and she dropped her gaze. Slowly, he slid toward her, relieved when she didn't flinch from him.

"I haven't kissed anyone like that, feeling it deep within my heart, since I went steady with Heather in high school."

"The captain of the cheerleading squad?" she whispered.

"Yeah. Though I like to think I'm more mature now than the boy I was then." He stared down at her hand and covered it with his. "I want to thank you for opening up and sharing some of your past with me. I know it wasn't easy, but it helps me understand you a little better now."

Shae looked at him then, gave a small nod and an even smaller smile. She seemed so vulnerable that it was all Keith could do not to take her in his arms and hold her. Powerless to resist, he put a finger underneath her chin, moved toward her, and touched his lips to hers in a brief, gentle kiss. It took every bit of determination he had to move away. The last thing he wanted was to scare her. Shallow waters were safest.

She opened wide, dark, ocean-deep eyes—ones he could easily drown in.

Keith swallowed and his voice came out a little husky. "I think we should call it a night, before I get hopelessly lost in those chocolate-colored eyes of yours and forget myself." He lightly stroked the back of his fingers over her cheek and managed a slight grin. "Chocolate always was one of my weaknesses."

Not willing to test his self-control further, he rose from the couch with a soft good night, leaving her staring after him in bewilderment.

❧

The next Sunday Shae was surprised when Keith woke early and accompanied her to church. He had exhibited an interest the previous afternoon at dinner, but she didn't think he'd really go. Not considering the way he'd been acting this past week. He'd spent little time with her, only seeing her during meals. And though those times had been pleasant, his attitude toward her apparently had altered. She wondered if the change had to do with her confession about never having dated. Although Keith's sudden distance was a relief, Shae also couldn't help but feel strangely disappointed.

From her place on the back pew of the historic church building, Shae noticed two young girls whisper and dart interested glances over their shoulders in his direction. Poor Keith. She wondered how he managed any semblance of a normal life.

After the service, he grabbed her arm and steered her out of the small church and to the car. The day was beautiful. The sun shone from a clear sky, and the sweet scent of wildflowers scattered over the grassy hills mixed with the ocean breeze. In the distance, between the budding trees and summer cottages, Shae could see a sliver of the Atlantic—cerulean blue today, instead of a stormy greenish gray.

However, yesterday's storm seemed to have invaded the confines of the car. Keith was quiet, and Shae sensed he was angry. He seemed morose, far away. Nothing like his usual self.

"It's not my fault," she said, breaking the silence.

"What?" He gave her a distracted glance.

"You looked at me as if I'd instigated the whole thing."

"What whole thing?"

"Today's message. I can't help it that Pastor Williams chose the topic of the prodigal son."

Keith didn't respond. Shae turned her upper body around in the bucket seat to get a better look at him. "You don't honestly believe I called him last night and asked him to change his message when I found out you were coming?"

He released a weary breath. "Of course not. I'm just going through a bit of a mental battle."

"Because of those girls back there?"

His brow creased. "What girls?"

Wow. He must have been deeply immersed in the message not to notice the interested stares he'd been getting.

"Never mind." Shae looked out the window, focusing on the scenery as they drove home. They passed a popular sandy beach, and Shae spotted several hardier souls throwing a football around and running along the sun-bleached dunes, though the temperature barely wavered above fifty. It had been an unusually cold spring.

"Freddie got in touch with *Teen Planet*," Keith said. "We've set the date up for a week from this Thursday. Okay with you?"

"Sure. My brother and his wife are coming to the island this week. They usually stay awhile, so there won't be any problem with me taking off a full day for the, uh, date." She still had a problem saying the word.

"Great." He glanced her way. "Did you tell your brother about me?"

"I didn't think you'd want your whereabouts known."

He softly snorted. "Don't you think he may begin to wonder when he sees me sitting on your porch?"

"Why should he? I own the inn, and you are my guest."

They rolled to a stop at a traffic light, and he turned to face her. "Is that all I am to you, Shae? Just a guest at The Roosting Place? I thought we'd gone beyond that."

His probing, flame-blue eyes melted her to her seat. This was getting dangerous as well as confusing. Hadn't he spent almost the entire past week practically ignoring her?

She shrugged and looked out the window. The car took off with a jerk, making the tires squeal.

Shae darted a glance in his direction, noting his tense jaw. "Even if I'd wanted to tell Tommy about you being here, there wasn't time," she explained. "It was a short call. My brother is a miser when it comes to money."

Keith gave a curt nod. Uncomfortable, Shae looked back out the window. When they reached the inn, she wrenched open her door and hurried from the car before he turned off the ignition.

⁂

"It's not over yet, Shae," Keith murmured as he watched her retreating figure in the rearview mirror. "I'm not going anywhere for awhile."

The relief Keith felt days ago that he'd successfully talked Freddie into putting off the contest date, so that Keith could extend his vacation, evaporated as frustration seized his emotions. He'd honestly thought he and Shae had reached an understanding. This past week he had done his level best to take their relationship slow and not push, not crowding her, and had foolishly thought he was making headway. So why was she holding back again? Keith knew she felt something for him. He'd seen it in her eyes. And since he'd come to this island, he couldn't stop thinking about her, couldn't stop wanting to be with her, even searching her out to do things with him that first week. Like a lovesick puppy.

Keith shook his head and shifted his gaze to the windshield and the blue sea—as changeable as Shae.

Perhaps it was time to switch tactics. Instead of treading carefully maybe he should pursue. That something from her past haunted her was obvious. And he was almost sure that *something* had to do with her parents. Was that what held her back from him?

He let out a mirthless chuckle. The situation was really ironic when he thought about it. Countless females threw themselves over each other to get to him. Yet the one woman Keith was interested in seemed bent on running the opposite direction.

Years ago he'd made a point to keep an emotional distance from women, though Heather had wanted to marry him right after high school. But Keith hadn't felt the same way. He didn't want any ties while trying to boost his singing career.

Thinking about those first years away from home, he felt shame flood through him, heating his face. He had eventually wised up and entered a drug rehab shortly after a good friend died from an overdose, and not long after that he'd sworn off promiscuous women. Yet could God ever forgive him for his temporary insanity? Was He really holding His arms open, waiting to forgive? Or did He have His back turned to Keith, as Keith imagined? Because he'd been raised in a Christian home, Keith knew the story of the prodigal son, had heard it many times when he was a kid. But he hadn't really understood the story then and wasn't sure he quite believed it now. . . .

While the mental and spiritual battle raged on inside him, Keith stared at the ocean and wondered if the expanse was too great to go to the other side.

❧

Shae darted a nervous glance Keith's way. Sunday morning she'd bolted from this car. Today was Wednesday. During that time Keith had completely avoided her, not even sharing in their meals, as he had done since he'd come to the inn. Shae had missed their dinner conversations—missed Keith—and that scared her. She didn't want to think of Keith as more than a guest. It was too dangerous.

"You're awfully quiet," Keith's voice broke into her musings.

She shrugged. "Not much to say."

Ha! What a joke. Her mind fairly screamed with questions she wanted answers to—answers only he could give. Why did he want to know so much about her? Why couldn't he leave her alone? Why had he ignored her? And then, after days of ignoring her, why did he suddenly appear and invite her on a picnic? Concentrating on the scenery, she tensed. Her eyes widened when she realized where they were headed.

To the left, dark brown clay bluffs stretched for miles along the south side of the island and sharply dropped 150 feet to the pale beaches below. Crimson and yellow wildflowers dotted the sparse shrubs, and wild grasses grew throughout the area. In the distance, an old red brick lighthouse with an A-shaped roof and octagonal tower stood sentinel against the powder-gray sky.

Keith drove a little farther then stopped the car. "This is as good a place as any. Let's eat." He reached behind him for the hamper.

Shae didn't move, barely breathed. "Who told you about this place?"

"No one needed to tell me, Shae. Mohegan's Bluffs is one of the biggest attractions on the island. I saw the write-up in a tourist brochure at the inn."

She chewed on her lip. "Let's go somewhere else. Please, Keith. It's. . .it's too cold to eat by the ocean, and I didn't bring a jacket."

"You can wear mine." He shrugged out of his bomber jacket and handed it to her.

"There are better places to have a picnic."

"I like it here," he countered stubbornly. "There's something about the ocean that speaks to you."

"Block Island has countless views of the ocean. We're completely surrounded by water. Why don't we go to Old Harbor, or the beach next to the inn—"

"I'm hungry now, and this is a great spot—one I haven't seen until today." Keith grinned. "Besides, I don't want to spend any more time driving around when that food in the hamper is begging for me to eat it." He got out of the car, putting an end to further argument.

Shae clutched the door handle tightly, wishing he hadn't taken the car keys. If she had the choice, she would drive off and leave him here. But she obviously had no choice.

Gritting her teeth, she got out of the car and slammed the door. She shrugged into Keith's jacket, smelling of spicy cologne, and trailed behind him. He had already spread a blanket on the ground. As Shae approached, he motioned her to it. She remained standing.

"Just listen to the soothing sound of that ocean," Keith said. "It's so peaceful here. Something I've really missed in my fast-paced life."

"It looks as if it might storm. I think we should go home."

"Storm? I don't think so. Not a thundercloud for miles." He handed her a sandwich. "Here. Eat up."

With a loud sigh, Shae knelt at the edge of the blanket and sat on her calves. She took the sandwich and paper cup he gave her, but didn't unwrap it. Just stared at a nearby clump of vegetation.

"Tiffany tells me you used to come here with your parents."

Her head shot up, anger eating away her unease. Tiffany!

"Oh? And what else did she tell you?" Shae squeezed the cup in her hand. It made a popping noise, and tea spilled out, sloshing over her fingers and onto her lap.

"Hey! You gotta be careful with those flimsy things. Here." Keith handed her a couple of napkins. "Good thing it wasn't hot coffee."

Shae automatically took the napkins, barely cognizant of the fact that her jeans leg was soaked. "What else did Tiffany tell you?" she demanded.

"That her times here were some of the best memories she had of her family," Keith said quietly after studying her a moment. "That your parents often took you to visit the light-house over there, and the beaches below—"

Shae rocketed to her feet. "That's it. I want to go home."

"I haven't finished eating yet."

"You know what? I really don't care."

Shae turned on her heel and stomped to the car. She'd only made it a few yards before she felt his hand on her shoulder, pulling her around to face him.

"What are you running from, Shae? I want to help. Please don't shut me out."

She shook his hand off, glaring at him. "Just because you're a big hotshot celebrity doesn't give you the right to interfere in my business. You act like some kind of shrink! Next thing you know you'll be wanting me to play some kind of word association game or some crazy thing like that."

"That might not be a bad idea," he said, as though considering.

"Oh, puh-leease. Give me a break." Shae spun on her heel, continued to the car, wrenched open her door, and got inside.

Keith slid behind the wheel, but made no move to put the key into the ignition. "Black."

Shae tensed. "Excuse me?"

"I'll say a word, and you quickly say the first word that comes to mind."

"You must be joking," Shae said, widening her eyes in disbelief. "Didn't you hear a word I said back there?"

"Black."

"What is it with all these games you keep coming up with? First twenty questions, then guessing games, now this!"

"Black."

Shae threw up her hands in disgust. "Okay, okay. If I humor you and play your stupid game, then can we go?"

"Black."

"White!" She looked daggers at him.

"Heaven," he shot back calmly.

"Hell."

"Bad."

"Good," she gritted between clenched teeth, throwing her head back against the seat.

"Life."

"Death."

"God."

"Powerful."

"Devil."

"Angel."

"Father."

"Mother."

"Sister."

"Brother."

"Daughter."

"Killer." The word slipped out, startling them both. Shae gaped, blinked. "I. . .I don't know why I said that. I—" She threw open her door and jumped outside.

Walk, just walk. Escape. She needed escape. He was getting too close. She had to calm down, get back in control. But she couldn't think straight, couldn't reason. This place. That day. Her legs moved automatically, the grasses swishing against her jeans. Her vision blurred with tears, making it harder to see.

"Shae!"

She heard him coming up behind her and increased her pace until she was almost at a run. Without her realizing it, her feet carried her toward the bluffs. He caught up to her, gripping her arm before she'd reached the barrier. "Shae—"

"Why can't you leave me alone?" she cried, whirling to face him. "Why don't you just go back to California and leave me alone?"

"I can't do that. I want to help you beat this thing."

"Why?! Why do you care?"

"I just do."

Beyond frustration, she put her hands straight up at shoulder level as though to ward him off. Staring at the ground, she shook her head and backed up until her tailbone hit the barrier.

"Shae," Keith said quietly. "I don't know much about your past, but I can guarantee you're no killer."

She clenched her teeth and glared at him. "How can you say that? You don't know anything about me!"

"I know enough to know you're not capable of such a thing."

Unable to handle his persistence any longer, she felt her last vestige of control snap. "Well, you're wrong," she screamed, the words rushing from her mouth before she could stop them. "You know nothing—nothing at all! Your manager was right. I am a killer! It's because of me my parents are dead. So now you know. There—are you happy now?"

She whirled from him and raced down the road.

seven

Stunned, Keith stood immobile and watched Shae run from him as if the hounds of hell were chasing her. Not for a minute did he believe she'd willfully killed anyone. Killers were angry or bitter, with hard hearts and selfish motives. Shae didn't fit the type. Yet at the same time Keith didn't deny the fact that *she* believed she'd killed her parents. How and why she felt that way, he hoped to find out some time in the future. But not today.

He moved to the car and slid behind the wheel. Slipping the key into the ignition, he started the car and pulled out onto the road in the direction Shae had taken.

As he came up alongside her, he eased his foot off the gas, hitting the switch that automatically rolled down the passenger window. She had trailed to a walk, her breath coming in panting gasps.

"Get in, Shae," he said, leaning across the seat.

She gave a short, hysterical laugh. "Sure you want. . .to ride with me. . .after what I said?"

"I'm sure."

She halted, darting him a puzzled, incredulous look. He put his foot on the brake.

"Why, Keith? Why don't you hate me now?"

Hate her? Keith studied her curiously. Her dark eyes held deep wells of pain. Wet, black trails ran down each cheek. His heart wrenched at her distress.

"I'm only going to say this once, Shae, and then I'm not going to speak of it anymore unless you bring it up." He released a soft breath, hoping he wasn't making a mistake that might send her over the edge again. "I know for some reason you feel responsible for your parents' deaths—and one day I

81

hope you'll trust me enough to tell me why. Until then, I plan to treat you as I always have. I'm a pretty good judge of character, believe it or not, and I think it's safe to say you're no murderer. Now, get inside, and I'll take you back to the inn. It's too far to walk."

Shae inhaled deeply, her eyes sliding shut a moment. At last, giving a curt nod, she opened the door and slid onto the passenger seat.

Relieved, Keith pulled the car away and headed toward the inn. The entire drive back, Shae kept her face averted, staring at the choppy ocean. The sky had grown a shade darker, and Keith was surprised when several raindrops splattered against the windshield. Soon the drops increased in quantity and strength, drumming against the car. He turned the wipers on.

"I didn't think it would rain, or I would have never suggested a picnic." He winced. *Great, Travers. You had to go and bring that up again.*

But Shae only shrugged. "New England weather," she said, her voice raspy. "Can't trust it. It'll pass soon enough."

She was right. By the time they reached the road leading to The Roosting Place, the downpour had abated.

Shae let out a groan.

"What's wrong?" Keith glanced her way.

"Tommy's car. I'd forgotten he was coming today." She pulled at her disheveled hair. "I can't face him looking like this!"

Keith nodded and turned the car onto another road.

Shae looked at him in surprise. "What are you doing?"

"Giving you time to compose yourself." He took a hand off the wheel, reached into his back pocket, and pulled out a comb, offering it to her. "I noticed there's a box of tissues on the backseat if you want to wipe your face."

When she didn't take the comb, he shot a glance her way. "Don't worry. I don't have cooties."

A grin trembled on the corners of her lips. "Thanks, Keith." Her soft words thanked him for so much more than the comb, and he gave her an understanding smile. She took the comb, put the visor down, and gasped when she saw her reflection in the mirror. Hurriedly she reached in back for the tissues and swiped one after another under her eyes, then took the comb and slowly worked it through the snarls in her thick hair.

While Shae spruced herself up, Keith drove along the road heading north toward the Great Salt Pond. From tourist brochures, he knew it was a sheltered harbor, a perfect retreat for water activities. At some point while he was here he'd like to check it out and do some boating. He missed that sport. Thinking about that made him think about his dad, and how he, Keith, and his older brother Kenneth would often take the sailboat out on summer weekends when Keith had been a kid. Life had been so simple then.

"Okay, I'm ready," Shae said, sticking the crumpled tissues into a car trash bag.

Without a word, Keith turned the car around. Soon they arrived at the inn. A slender man with black hair stood on the veranda, his hands in his pockets.

"That's Tommy," Shae said nervously. "Will I pass inspection? He's sometimes a little overbearing in the protective brother role, and I don't want him to suspect I've been upset."

Keith drove to the side of the inn, put the car in park, and turned off the ignition before looking her way. She stared back, her eyes apprehensive. Her ebony hair was smooth, framing a face that was a shade too pale. Pink bands stood out on her cheeks where she'd rubbed hard with the tissues. His heart lurched with empathy at what she must be going through. He lifted a hand and, with his thumb, wiped away an overlooked black speck near her jaw.

"Just one more thing. Smile. And remember, I'm right behind you." He gave her an encouraging grin and was relieved when the corners of her mouth lifted in response.

❧

"There you are! I was worried when you didn't meet us at the ferry. Who's this?"

Shae tried to keep the smile on her face, though it was diffi-cult with Tommy's suspicious stare settling on her, traveling to Keith, then shooting back to her again.

Before she could reply, Tiffany came sailing out the door, a triumphant expression on her face. "See, I told you, Linda. Keith Travers is so Shae's boyfriend."

Embarrassed heat rushed to Shae's face. "Tiffany—"

"Tiff, you're too old for these kinds of games," Linda's voice grew louder as she approached the door and stepped outside. Her blue eyes lit on Keith and widened. "Oh, wow. . . ."

Shae wished she could dissolve into the ground and disap-pear between the tufts of wet grass. Somehow she had to make it through introductions. She felt Keith move closer, as though to offer support, and it bolstered her to speak.

"Tommy, Linda, this is Keith. Keith, my brother and my sister-in-law."

Tommy shook Keith's hand in a death grip, giving him a long, measured look. Linda talked as if she'd been medicated and didn't have proper use of her tongue or brain. Embarrassed by the behavior of her kin, Shae grimaced and suggested they all go to the family parlor.

Gretta brought coffee, and Shae gratefully cupped the hot ceramic, taking measured sips as she listened to Tommy's pointed and nosy questions. This was ridiculous. He sounded as if he were trying out for the part of Perry Mason. Just what had Tiffany told her brother to make him act this way?

Shae had to hand it to Keith. He took it well. Casually he answered each question, not once getting upset. If it had been Shae who was being grilled like a defendant on a witness stand, she wouldn't be half as congenial.

"A contest date, huh?" Tommy darted a glance Shae's way. "Sounds fishy to me. Who dreamed up something like that?"

Shae rolled her eyes. "It's perfectly legit."

"Shae's right," Tiffany piped up. "I should know. I filled out the form."

"*You* filled out the form?" Tommy's eyes narrowed as he

looked from Tiffany to Keith and back to Shae.

Linda broke out of the stupor she'd been in since meeting Keith, rose from her chair, and put an arm around her husband's shoulders. "Tommy, let's talk about this later. We just got here. Shae's a smart girl. I'm sure she wouldn't get involved in anything that was in any way suspect."

Tommy hesitated, then gave her a faint smile and linked an arm around her waist. "Okay, Hon."

"I need your help with the luggage," Linda said moving with him to the door. "That suitcase sticks and I can never open it." Before they disappeared from sight, Linda looked over her shoulder, flashing a conspiratorial smile at Shae.

"Man, what's with him?" Tiffany said when they were out of earshot. "I don't think I've ever seen him give anyone the third degree like that."

Shae lifted a brow. "So just what did you tell him while we were gone?"

"Nothing, really." Tiffany perked up, sitting forward in the chair. "Hey, guess what? Tommy wants to go to Mohegan Bluffs this Sunday. I haven't been there in forever!"

"This Sunday?" Shae said faintly, setting down the coffee before she spilled it.

"Yeah. We're going after church. Oh, wow, I better call Liz and let her know. Tommy said she could come too." Tiffany bounded off the chair and out the door.

"You okay?" Keith asked quietly when the sudden silence in the room threatened to smother her.

Shae took a deep breath and nodded. "It shouldn't have come as a shock. Tommy often goes there with Tiffany when he comes to visit." Her gaze briefly lowered to her lap. "About my brother—I'm sorry about that cross-examination you got. My guess is he acted that way because I've never dated. And to hear that my first date is with you probably rattled him."

"I understand. No need to apologize. He cares about you and wants to make sure my intentions are honorable. If I were at home I'd do the same with my three sisters, though Beth is still the baby in the family and I won't have to worry about her social life for a long time."

Keith hesitated, looked at his coffee. "Shae, about this Sunday. . ."

She tensed.

"I wasn't going to say anything, since I thought you'd spend the day with your brother and his wife. But my guess is you won't be going with them." He looked at her. "Right?"

"Right."

"Then I'd like you to come with me. I'm going home for a visit."

Startled at the unexpected announcement, she drew a breath, her eyes widening. "Really, Keith?"

He nodded. "And it would mean a lot to me if you came along. I could use the support," he joked, though his blue eyes were serious.

She hesitated. "Are you sure your parents won't mind?"

"When my mom discovers that it was largely because of your influence that I decided to see them, I imagine she'll roll out the red carpet for you."

Shae smiled. "Then the answer is yes. I'd like to go with you and meet your family."

꙰

The evening progressed better than the afternoon had. Shae's brother was sullen, but he didn't question Keith further or stare at him as if he were a convicted felon. Linda made up for Tommy's morose attitude with her bubbly behavior, shooting Keith question after question—none of them as uncomfortable or rude as Tommy's had been.

When dinnertime came, they went to the dining room to catch the floor show. Seeing a rather large crowd, Keith slipped on his sunglasses then took them off, deciding in this dark room they made him look conspicuous. Besides, from what he could tell, the audience consisted of those from an older generation. Keith doubted anyone in this crowd had even heard of him.

Feeling at ease, he gave his order to the waitress who'd come to their table. After she left, he settled back and listened to the singer. She crooned a couple of blues songs from the forties while a man in a black tuxedo expertly accompanied her on the piano.

Keith took a sip of rich coffee. The duo was good, but he preferred Shae's bell-like soprano to this woman's husky alto. He leaned over to make a comment, when he noticed Freddie enter the dining room and survey the area with that predatory expression on his face. *Uh-oh. Now what?*

Freddie's gaze landed on Keith and he motioned him over.

"I'll be right back," Keith whispered to Shae. As he walked away, he noticed the waitress approach the table with their food, and barely withheld a groan.

"Do you have built-in radar?" he asked in a low voice when he'd reached his manager. "Is that how you can tell when I'm about to eat?"

"Come on," Freddie said, grabbing his arm. "This is more important than food."

They walked out the door, down a hallway, and slipped into an empty room. Freddie flicked on the light to expose three washers and two dryers on a white linoleum floor.

Keith shrugged his arm away. "You brought me here to do laundry?"

Freddie ignored his feeble joke. "I was on the phone with my secretary earlier, and she mentioned that you only have two months under the old contract. We need to get a new one made up."

"Yeah, okay."

Freddie's eyes narrowed. "You don't sound too sure, Travers." Without waiting for Keith's response, he added, "It was rumored Hugh Fielder from FLD Management was seen talking to you the night of the Video Music Awards. He make you any offers?"

Keith let out an irritated breath. "Yeah. But don't worry about it. I didn't like his terms—"

"Of all the—" Freddie let loose with a few choice expletives. "That rotten, no good chiseler. . .trying to steal my people when my back is turned—"

"I told you, I turned him down. So just chill."

But Freddie wouldn't be pacified. "As soon as this 'dream date' is over, we're heading back to California ASAP. I should have never let you talk me into pushing the date to a later day and staying here so long in the first place. The date is set for next Thursday. We leave on Friday." He clamped down on his unlit cigar and turned on his heel, leaving the room.

Keith's eyes slid shut. Friday. He had known he would have to return to California soon. Yet now that a definite day had been set, an uncomfortable heaviness settled in his gut. It would be difficult to leave this relaxing island paradise. But it would be even harder to say good-bye to Shae.

❧

The next morning, shortly after breakfast, Keith knocked on Shae's open office door. "Hey, there. Want to take an hour or two off, rent a couple of bikes, and hit the trails?"

Startled, Shae studied him. Obviously, her hysterical confession at the bluffs hadn't fazed him one bit. Like he'd told her he would, Keith treated her the same as always, as if the incident had never happened. But it had.

True, she hadn't outright killed her parents, but she was responsible for their deaths. And that horrible blotch could never be erased from her life, or her records. God could never forgive her for what she'd done.

Feeling that awful blackness rise inside, Shae knew she needed escape. Sunshine. Fresh air. A change of surroundings.

"Sure," she said, rising and throwing her pen down on her open ledger, "but we don't need to rent bikes. I've got several here. I'll meet you on the porch in five minutes."

She went upstairs and changed into some old jeans, a sweatshirt, and sneakers. Before she left the inn, she told Gladys, the assistant manager, that she would be gone. Linda was in bed, not feeling well, and Tommy was taking a walk through town.

With Keith's help, Shae retrieved two bikes from the storage shed, wondering how long it had been since she'd been cycling. They pedaled down a nearby twisting trail close to the water, abreast of each other. The sea breeze was cool, the salt spray invigorating. A pale sun shone in a crystal blue sky, the ocean shimmering a darker blue below.

The path took them through a nearby copse of trees. When they approached a freshwater pond, Keith suggested they stop for a breather. Shae gladly agreed, her leg muscles beginning to ache. She climbed off her bike, leaned it against a tree trunk next to his, and joined him where he sat sprawled on the grass, against a maple, one hand dangling over his upraised knee.

For a few minutes they relaxed in undisturbed silence, listening to the rhythmic birdsong filtering through the trees. Keith reached into his pocket and pulled out a small foil bag, tore it open with his teeth, and offered it to her.

"Peanuts?"

"Thanks." Shae held out a hand, and he poured several into her palm. She smirked in amusement.

"What's so funny?" he asked suspiciously.

"I was just thinking. Have you noticed—it seems whenever we get together, food is involved?"

Keith grinned, leaning his head back against the tree trunk. "I hadn't really thought about it, but you're right. Guess it's because my manager starves me, so naturally it's uppermost in my mind."

She eyed his slim, well-built physique and healthy skin tone. "Yeah, you really look starved."

He popped a couple of peanuts into his mouth. "By the way, I called Mom, and she's excited about meeting you. We'll charter a flight from the airport to the mainland and rent a car—"

"A plane? Can't we take the ferry?" Shae asked, feeling the blackness rise again.

"A plane trip will take twelve minutes," Keith said patiently. "The ferry takes over an hour."

She looked down, brushing imaginary dirt from her jeans. "I know. But I'd prefer to take the ferry. I don't like to fly. That way we can take my car."

"Don't you think it's a little too late to get a reservation for taking the car on the ferry?"

"We can go on standby," she countered. "At least we can try. . . ."

A long pause. "Okay, Shae. If that's what you want, that's what we'll do."

She gave him a self-conscious smile. "Thanks, Keith. I appreciate it."

He didn't return her smile. His steady eyes regarded her, probing, asking questions he didn't speak. Afraid of his starting another inquisition into her past, Shae rose from the ground. "I need to be getting back. More tourists mean more work. This time of year the ferries deliver thousands of people to the island a day—though they don't all spend the night here, of course. There wouldn't be room for them, since the island is only seven miles long and three miles wide—and our town of New Shoreham is the smallest town in the nation." She gave a nervous laugh, realizing she sounded a lot like an overeager tour guide.

Keith nodded thoughtfully, watching her. "All right. Let's go."

On the trail again, he glanced her way as they pedaled out of the copse. "I'll race you," he challenged with a wide smile.

"Race me?" She barely got the words out before he took off, his feet pumping hard on the pedals.

Shae shook her head, bemused, and then began pedaling harder to catch up. Him and his endless games! He was nothing but a big kid.

As they neared the inn, she came closer to him, by this time panting for breath. She was in no shape for these long-distance bike races of his! Perspiration trickled down her face, and she was thankful she'd thought to gather her hair back in a looped ponytail before leaving the inn.

She won by a narrow margin and practically fell off her

bike when she dismounted. Her legs no longer felt a part of her. Bending over, she grasped her knees, gasping for air. Keith's footsteps crunched her way.

"Congratulations. You won."

She raised her head to see him grinning, his arms crossed. To her disgust, he wasn't even breathing heavily. "Small consolation. . .if I don't live to enjoy the prize," she rasped.

"Prize?" Keith asked in mock amazement. "You expect a prize? Hmm. Okay, tell you what. Since I lost, I'll put up the bikes."

Skeptical about his jocular behavior, Shae watched as he pushed both bicycles into the shed and closed the door. She straightened as he came toward her.

"And since you're the winner," he said quietly, searching her face, "you know what you get, don't you?"

Shae felt mesmerized by the look in his eyes. "No. What?"

"This."

Placing a hand to either side of her face, he inclined his head and kissed her, stealing what little breath she'd regained. Though the kiss was feather light, her heart sped up again, and her legs threatened to fold beneath her.

"Shae!"

Tommy's gruff voice sliced through the pleasant wooziness cottoning her mind. She tore her lips from Keith's warm ones, blinking up at him, then turned to face her brother.

He stood near the inn, his stance angry. "We need to talk. Now." His dark eyes cut into Keith. "If you'll excuse us?"

Disturbed at being caught kissing Keith, but even more upset by her brother's Neanderthal behavior, Shae frowned.

"It's okay," Keith murmured behind her, speaking so only she could hear. He put a reassuring hand on her shoulder. "I'll talk to you later."

Shae watched as he strode toward the inn. When Keith neared Tommy, her brother caught his gaze, his eyes clearly issuing a warning. Keith paused then continued walking toward the front. After he disappeared from sight, Shae snapped her gaze to Tommy's.

"Just what is your problem?"

His eyes narrowed. "I might ask you the same thing. One minute you show no interest in men, the next minute you're a groupie." He said the last word as if it left a bitter taste in his mouth.

Shae's cheeks grew even hotter. "You have no idea what you're talking about. And I suggest we leave it that way. This is my life—not yours."

Wanting only to escape, she stormed toward the inn. He caught her elbow when she would have swept past. "I care, big sister, even if you don't. I don't want to see you get hurt. You have no experience in this kind of thing, and with this Keith guy, you're jumping into the major leagues instead of starting with Little League and learning how to bat first."

Shae rolled her eyes at Tommy's reference to his favorite sport. "All right, Tommy, point taken. I'll be careful. Now if that's all, I really need to get back to work—"

"No, that's not what I needed to talk to you about."

Shae's heart jumped at the change in his pitch. Low, serious, as if he had something important to say, and she wouldn't want to hear it. She looked at him. His dark eyes were solemn.

"Let's go sit on the porch and talk. We have some things we need to discuss."

eight

Shae sank to a cushioned chair on the wraparound porch and expectantly turned to face her brother, who'd taken the seat next to her. "Well?"

"Linda's pregnant."

Shae gaped, then offered a faint grin. "Congratulations." When he didn't respond, she studied him in confusion, her smile fading. "So what's the problem? Babies are good news, right?"

He gave a curt nod, his gaze going to the trees. "There are... complications. You know she had a miscarriage last year...," he broke off, swept an unsteady hand through his hair. "Bottom line is the doctor said that Linda needs plenty of rest, even after the baby comes. She needs someone to help out."

Shae's breath snagged in her throat. She had a feeling she knew where this was going. "So, you're going to hire a nurse?" she said hopefully. "Or a maid?"

"No." Tommy looked at her then. "I want Tiffany to come live with us."

Shae stared at him for a few seconds, then rocketed up from her chair. Moving to the railing, she kept her gaze fixed on the ocean. Tense, she clutched the white banister. "We've discussed this before, Tommy. Tiffany stays with me."

"Why, Shae? I love her, too."

Shae's grip tightened on the carved wood. How could she tell Tommy that his wife was just too immature to raise a teenager? Not that Shae was doing the greatest job of it, but Linda was two years younger than Shae and acted more like a teenybopper than an adult. Their parents would have wanted the best for Tiffany. Shae was determined to see that wish come to fulfillment.

She turned on her heel and made her way to the door.

"Case closed, Tommy. It's best for everyone concerned."

"She could die, Shae."

Tommy's quiet words halted her as she put her hand to the brass latch. Stunned, she looked at him. "What?"

"Linda. She could die."

Shae shook her head. "With the wonders of modern medicine on her side?"

"She has a weak heart. They were discussing the probability of her needing a pacemaker, but now that she's pregnant. . ."

A weak heart? Linda? Sweet, vivacious, bubbly Linda? Shae's eyes slid shut.

"Don't tell her I told you. She doesn't want anyone to know. Just please think about Tiffany coming back with us to Connecticut. She would love it on the farm. There's a good school nearby and plenty of wide-open space. Not a lot of opportunity for her to get into trouble. . ."

The pleading note in his voice combined with the worried look in his eyes stabbed into Shae. She turned her gaze toward the door. "I'll think about it," she murmured. "And, Tommy. . .I'm sorry about Linda."

She knew she should go hug him, offer some kind of comfort, but the roller coaster of emotions she'd whirled through these past weeks made her seek the solace of her locked office instead. How much more could she take? First Keith pops into her lonely life with his crazy games—knocking her off balance and causing her to tell him more than she should. . .not to mention his unexpected warm kisses catching her off guard and making her melt like a marshmallow in a flame, then Tiffany shaking up life with her unpredictable ways followed by Tommy's news of Linda. And now Tommy wanted to take her sister away from her. Hadn't she been robbed of enough in life—even if it was her own fault?

Shae dropped her face into her open hands, wondering what to do. Knowing what she should do.

એ

Sunday dawned bright, and after early morning services, Keith and Shae hurried to catch the ferry. They hadn't been able to get a spot for Shae's car, but Keith assured her they could rent one at Port Judith.

Twenty minutes later, they sat on the third level of the sleek white ferry that chugged across the ocean. The crisp sea breeze kissed Shae's face and hair, and she deeply inhaled the familiar and loved salty smell. Seagulls screeched, and she watched them dip and sway, their white wings vivid against the washed-out blue of the sky.

During the entire trip over to the mainland, Keith was talkative—more so than usual—and he gestured with his hands a lot. The usual sunglasses were in place, and so far his anonymity was protected. However, once they hit Port Judith and rented a car for the day, he became more pensive, frowning as he drove. He gripped the steering wheel, his knuckles white.

"Keith?" He looked her way, and she offered an encouraging smile. "Everything will be fine, I'm sure. You said your mother was happy to hear from you and was looking forward to today."

Keith nodded, turning his gaze back to the windshield, but the grim look remained. "It isn't Mom I'm worried about. It's Dad." He puckered his cheeks, blowing out a noisy breath. "Like I said, we didn't exactly part on good terms. I basically left home, but he pretty much threw me out at the same time. Said if I wanted to ruin my life, he wouldn't stand by and watch." His low, emotional words clearly revealed to Shae just how much he loved his dad.

"Four years is a long time," she said gently. "I'm sure by now he's forgotten the trouble between you and is looking forward to the visit as much as your mom is."

Keith didn't look her way. . .didn't say anything.

"Tell me again about your sisters," Shae said, changing the subject, hoping to get his mind off the problem.

Keith was quiet a moment, clearly lost in thought. "Abby, the oldest, is a little boy-crazy. She should be fresh out of high school by now, if I remember right. And Candy wears braces, which are a real issue with her from what Mom wrote me several years back. Try not to notice them. Bethie's the youngest. She collects Barbie dolls and every accessory that goes with them." He chuckled. "She's probably got the complete town by now."

"They sound like a nice group of girls."

"They are. I have a brother too—Kenneth—but he had duty this weekend. He's in the Navy, stationed in Virginia Beach. One of these days I'd sure like to see him again."

"I hope that happens for you, Keith. I really do. Family is so important."

He gave a vague nod, thoughtful once more. "Shae, there's something I suppose I should tell you. Generally when someone wins a contest, it's up to them to meet with the company holding the contest. When I found out the winner was from Rhode Island and only a short distance from my hometown, I insisted on coming. Freddie wasn't too happy about it. But like I said, I sometimes get the final word."

"Then you'd planned to visit your family all along?" she asked in mild shock.

"Yeah, though I chickened out several times since I've been here." He briefly looked her way. "Your advice that morning I found you dusting really had an impact on me, though—made me think. Thank you for that."

Shae smiled. "I'm glad I could help."

"More than you know."

The drive was long, but Shae didn't mind. She enjoyed being with Keith. Now that much of her past had been laid before this man—and he hadn't rejected her—it was easier to relax around him. He still didn't know everything, nor did she plan to tell him. There was no reason to. He would be leaving for California soon.

The thought invaded like a thundercloud on a clear day.

❧

Keith turned onto a narrow residential street lined with colorful clapboard houses and pulled the car to a stop in front of a yellow one. Hollyhocks climbed the front wall and porch rail. Flowered curtains fluttered in the open windows. In the yard, a giant elm stood sentinel, a tire swing hanging from its lower branch.

Keith sucked in his lower lip. This was it.

The door flew open and a blond girl holding a toddler on one hip ran out to greet them. "Keith! You really came!"

Before he was all the way out of the car, he was engulfed in a bear hug, baby and all. When his sister pulled away, he looked down at her in shock. "Abby? Wow! You look great. I'm glad to see you put on some weight—you always were too skinny. But why are you baby-sitting on Sunday?"

Abby laughed and hefted the slipping baby higher on her hip. "I'm not, Dummy. This is Ricky." She looked at the chubby baby, then at Keith. "Say hi to your nephew."

"My nephew," Keith echoed, dumbfounded.

"Sure. Didn't you get Mom's letters? I married Matt three years ago—"

"Ab-by!" A desperate masculine shout bellowed from within the house, interrupting her.

"Oops. Sandra must need a diaper change. I'd recognize that frantic tone in Matt's voice any day. I still haven't convinced him to help with that chore, though he does with all the others," Abby explained hurriedly, as she walked back up the stairs. "Come on in. Don't be a lug and stand out here all day." She disappeared into the house.

"Are you okay?" Shae asked softly, putting a hand to his arm.

Keith nodded, but he wasn't sure if he was. Why didn't he remember reading about Abby getting married? Three years ago. . .must have been during his first European tour. His stint with drugs and drinking had probably aided in his forgetfulness too. Or maybe he was just dense. He honestly didn't remember reading about Abby's marriage.

Making an effort to compose himself, he threw a faint grin Shae's way and walked with her up the sidewalk. Before they reached the door, a tiny woman wearing a huge smile rushed out to greet them.

"Keith!" She hurtled into his arms.

"Mom?" He hugged her close. After a long moment, she pulled away, her blue eyes watery. Gray hairs had replaced most of the blond ones, and her face had more wrinkles. With a pang of worry, he noted she looked tired. "You okay?" he asked, putting an arm around her shoulders.

"I am now that you came."

Keith smiled, wiped her tears away with his thumb then looked at Shae. "This is Shae Stevens, Mom. The girl I told you about."

His mom turned to Shae, taking one of Shae's hands in both of hers. "What a pleasure to meet you! Keith told me that his being here is largely due to you. I want to thank you from the bottom of my heart, though there are no words to express how grateful I am for this day—" She broke off, her words wobbly.

"Don't mind my family. They're all a bit overemotional," Keith said with a wink to Shae.

"Oh, you!" Keith's mother playfully struck her son's shoulder. "Well, come on inside. Dinner won't be for another thirty minutes, but I've got chips and pretzels, and I can open a can of salted nuts—"

"Mom," Keith said softly, "don't fuss. We'll be fine until dinner." He sobered. "Dad around?"

"He's reading the paper. You know how your father likes to keep informed."

Keith reached for Shae's hand as they walked into the cozy mulberry and tan den scattered with appliqués and doilies of all sizes. His father looked up from where he sat in a recliner, a pair of reading glasses perched on the end of his nose. He stood, setting down the newspaper, and eyed Keith with weary blue eyes.

"Hello, Keith," he said, no sign of animosity in his tone.

"Dad." Keith barely got the greeting out. His father had

aged, though he must only be in his early fifties. Yet the wheat-colored hair was almost white, and numerous lines Keith didn't remember covered most of his face. He looked as if life had beaten him.

He extended a gnarled hand, and Keith took it in an awkward handshake. Both men tried to hold emotion back, but failed, and his father pulled Keith into a strong embrace. "It's good to have you home, Son."

The low, emphatic words unleashed a few drops of wetness, and Keith swiped a hand over his cheeks to rid them of tears while he pulled away. "It's good to be home, Dad."

A young teenager, whom Keith guessed to be Tiffany's age, strode into the room. She flashed a faint tin smile, braces covering her teeth. "Hi," she said a little nervously.

"Candy!" Keith moved to hug his sister. "You've hardly changed. Except your hair is curlier and lighter than it was." He was relieved to find someone who had stayed pretty much the same since he'd left. "Too much sun, or are you using hair color? It's pretty," he added hastily, seeing her cheeks and forehead go pink.

"I'm Beth."

"Bethie?" he whispered, his eyes going wide. "But when I left, you were playing with Barbie dolls and had freckles and braids." His gaze swept over her and he noted the curves underneath the striped T-shirt and baggy jeans. On second glance at her face he noticed she was wearing makeup too.

She wrinkled her nose in a saucy way. "Get real, Keith. I'm too old to play with dolls now."

"Yes, I can see that." His voice was strained. "So, how old are you?"

"I turned fourteen last winter. You do remember my birthday is a week before Christmas, don't you?" she asked tartly.

"Bethany Anne Travers—we'll have none of that," his father said. "Apologize to your brother."

She sighed and rolled her eyes. "Sorry, Keith. I'm really glad you found time to visit. I need to go back to the kitchen and finish making the salad now. Later."

She pranced from the room, and Keith sank onto the couch, every part of him feeling the shock. Shae took a place beside him. "You okay?" she asked, looping her hand around his arm and leaning close.

"I don't know." Keith sat perched on the edge of the sofa, staring at the floor, his forearms resting on his thighs. "So much has changed."

"Beth has developed an attitude this past year," his father explained. "Don't mind her, Son."

The front door banged open, and a beautiful woman with wheat blond hair and bright blue eyes rushed into the room, followed by a dark-haired man who eyed Keith with awe. He already knew who the girl was. He only had three sisters. But if he hadn't known for certain, Keith would've never believed the elegant young woman standing in front of him in the chic designer suit was Candy.

"Keith!" She ran to him, knelt on the floor and hugged him hard.

"Hi, Candy," he murmured, giving her a limp hug back. "You've changed. You're a real knockout now."

"Uh, thanks—I think," Candy said uncertainly, her straight white teeth, minus the braces, flashing in a pretty smile. "I want you to meet Carl." She looked with adoration at the man beside her. "We are going to be married at the end of the year. I hope you can come to the wedding, Keith."

Keith soundlessly formed the word "married," then shook his head. "Yeah, sure," he said, not really knowing what he was saying. Too much was happening too fast, and he needed to get away. "If you guys will excuse me for a minute, I'll be right back."

He offered Shae a faint smile then strode from the sofa and onto the back porch. Inhaling the pungent air fragrant with the scent of his mother's rosebushes, he closed his eyes. Well, at least one thing hadn't changed—his mother's love of roses.

Walking around to the side of the house where the old oak

stood, he studied the high leafy branches. He almost gave a sigh of relief to see the old tree house—rotting, and minus wooden planks—but still there. Seeing his childhood refuge brought comfort. He almost wished he were a kid again and could escape into the private world he and Kenneth had shared. What fun they'd had! Pretending to be pirates hiding treasure. . .frequently peering between branches and looking for enemy ships dotting the wide ocean.

Keith shook his head. How time flew. It seemed like only yesterday they'd been troublesome boys playing pranks. Like the soap that turned the skin black. That had happened on a Sunday morning, and the family had been late to church because of it. Keith and Kenneth hadn't been able to sit down for some time after that.

A finger tapped his shoulder, breaking into his reverie, and he turned. Feminine arms wrapped around his neck, and a curvy body pressed close while a pair of soft lips landed on his in a kiss that sizzled. Bewildered by the past twenty minutes, as well as the present few seconds, Keith did nothing, feeling powerless to stop the kiss that might have lasted a few seconds or an eternity for all he knew. When she pulled away, he looked down into a pair of sea-green eyes.

"Welcome home, Keith."

"Heather."

She tried to kiss him again, but he stepped back.

Heather's brows drew down into a frown. "Aren't you happy to see me?"

"Sure," Keith said uneasily. "You've changed."

And she had, though he probably would have recognized her. The ponytail and cheerleading outfits were gone, of course, but the woman standing in front of him looked like she could have stepped off the cover of a high fashion magazine. A long-sleeved green top hugged full curves and was cut low enough to leave little to the imagination and high enough to give a glimpse of her tanned midriff. Slim-fitting pants revealed she was still model-thin. She wore three-inch stacked heels, making her legs seem even longer. Sunny blond hair swirled around her shoulders in the latest style.

She was beautiful, but Keith wasn't tempted.

As if Heather could read his mind, her eyes hardened. "What's the matter, Keith? Now that you're a big celebrity, I'm not good enough for you anymore?" She stepped toward him and looked up coyly, her hand going to his chest. "Why don't you give me a chance? I've missed you. Maybe I don't have as much experience as those glamorous stars you've dated. But I'm willing to learn." She trailed a coral fingernail down the middle of his chest.

Grabbing her hand hard, he stopped its trek.

"Ow! You're hurting me." She looked up and bit her lower lip when she saw his angry gaze.

"You're a little old to play with fire, aren't you, Heather?"

"What do you mean?"

"Stop trying to act like something you're not. And why are you wearing *that?* It's not even your style."

She smiled. "Do you like it? I wore it especially for you."

"No. It makes you look cheap."

She pouted. "What's wrong with you, anyway? We're not innocent kids playing at love anymore. We're supposed to be two adults. So why don't you treat me like one?" She moved closer. "You might even find you like it."

Keith gripped her upper arms, pushing her back. "I didn't come home to rekindle a high school romance. There's someone else in my life."

He saw the hurt flash in her eyes and felt instant remorse for his gruff behavior. They had known each other for years, played on the same street, grown up together.

"Heather, I know I left without saying good-bye, and I'm sorry. It wasn't very nice of me. But we had already drifted apart—"

"Who is she?"

He blew out a breath. "It doesn't really matter, okay? It's been over four years. There were no promises made between us."

"Is she here today? Is that her car out front?"

"Keith?"

His mother's voice came clearly to them before she rounded the corner. Keith quickly stepped away from his former girlfriend.

"Oh, hello, Heather. I didn't know you were here."

"Hi, Mrs. Travers."

"Why don't you come in and say hello to everyone? It's been awhile since we've seen you," his mother said, to Keith's chagrin. The last thing he wanted was for Heather and Shae to meet. He had enough problems trying to gain Shae's trust. This could spoil everything.

Keith firmly took Heather's upper arm, pointing her in the direction of her house. "I think Heather has to go home now—"

"Oh, don't be silly, Keith," she purred, smiling up at him. "I can come in for a minute just to say hi. Besides, I'd love to meet your *girlfriend.*"

"Well, then, that's settled," his mother said. "Come along, Heather."

Heather broke away from his grasp, and Keith watched the two women walk ahead of him. Shaking his head in dismay, he had little choice but to follow.

nine

Shae politely pretended to listen to Carl give an elaborate account of the house he and Candy had found, her mind all the while wondering what had happened to Keith. He'd been gone a long time.

The back door opened, and she looked up. A voluptuous blond glided in beside Keith's mom. Keith followed. Shae's eyes widened. The coral dots in the pattern of his gray sweater matched his lips. Was he wearing lipstick? Taking another look at the blond, Shae solved the mystery.

Her heart seemed to freeze into a chunk of ice. Tommy had warned her she was playing in the major leagues. Shae knew how popular Keith was with women. If she hadn't listened, it was her own fault.

"Heather," Candy said, obviously uneasy, "what are you doing here?"

Heather. The cheerleading captain. Of course.

"Just wanted to say hi to my old friends." She turned narrowed green eyes on Shae. "Hello. I don't believe we've met."

"Shae Stevens." Her voice came out strained.

"Heather Fontaine." With graceful ease, she covered the distance and perched on a chair across from the couch. "So tell me, Shae, how did you meet Keith? Are you one of his fans?"

Keith strode their way. "Heather, I don't think—"

Candy shot up from the couch. "Keith, can I talk to you a minute? Excuse us." She grabbed his arm and escorted him from the room as though she were a jailer taking a prisoner to his cell.

Shae looked on in confusion. *What was that all about?*

Carl cleared his throat and asked Keith's father if he'd like to check out his new car. Agreeing, the older man hastily stood, and the pair left the room.

Heather's gaze roamed Shae's face, hair, and rose-colored silk dress, and she gave her a smile that didn't quite reach her eyes. "I hope you didn't think my question rude, Shae. But, well, you see, I've known Keith a long time. As a matter of fact, we went steady in high school all through our junior and senior years, and I've really been looking forward to seeing him again—"

Abby rounded the corner, carrying Ricky. "Heather! It's been ages." She gave her a quick hug. "Come and see the baby. Come on. She looks just like a little doll when she's asleep."

Heather rose and went with Abby, though it was obvious she didn't want to. Keith strode back into the room, minus the lipstick on his mouth and wearing a sheepish expression on his face.

Shae dropped her gaze to a pile of boating magazines on the table. He sank to the cushion beside her. "Shae, about Heather—"

"Dinner's ready!" Keith's mom singsonged from the open kitchen door. "Where is everybody?"

"Mr. Travers and Carl went to check out Carl's new car," Shae said in a monotone. "I think the ladies are looking at the baby."

"Oh. Well, come along you two. I'll get the others." The woman whisked out the front door.

Keith put a hand over Shae's clasped ones resting on her knees. "Shae, as I was saying. . ."

Beth breezed into the room from the kitchen. "Have either of you two seen Abby?"

Shae pulled her hands away from Keith and motioned to the hallway beyond. Once the girl headed that direction, Keith spoke again. "I'm not sure what you're thinking, but I can guess. Shae, it's not how it looks—"

The front door swung open and Keith's mom, dad, and Carl piled inside. "Come on you two," Keith's mom said, gesturing with her arm. "Don't want the food to get cold."

Keith blew out a short, irritated breath. "We'll talk later. This isn't over."

Shae turned her head and looked directly into his eyes. "Yes, Keith. I think maybe it is."

❧

Silence shrouded the car. Keith had tried several times to explain about Heather, but each time Shae focused her attention out her window at the passing scenery. Although the last time he'd tried to explain, she did give a brief nod—not encouraging, but at least it showed she was listening. Frustrated, he concentrated on the road and mentally reviewed the disastrous day.

Not all bad, he relented. Being reunited with his family—especially his father—had been worth any embarrassment or frustration Keith had suffered. After dinner, his dad had taken him aside and they'd had a long talk. Though no mention was made of Keith's career, his father treated Keith as though no harsh words had ever been spoken between them—even suggesting that the next time Keith made it to Rhode Island they go sailing.

And Keith planned to visit again. As often as he could. The shock of seeing the changes in his family made Keith realize he didn't want to miss out on their lives any more than he had to. He shouldn't have been surprised at the differences, since he, too, had changed in four years. Yet he'd kept a mental picture of the way they'd been when he left, expecting to see that same picture today.

Loud inhaling followed by a melodic hum alerted Keith that Shae had fallen asleep. He smiled. She really did have a musical snore.

At the docks they took back the rental and barely made it to the ferry in time for its scheduled departure. Once aboard, Keith turned to Shae. "Did you have a good nap?"

Her eyes narrowed in suspicion. "Fair. Why do you ask?"

"Oh, no reason." She was still testy, and Keith decided now was not the time for banter.

Instead he filled the hour talking about his family and was relieved when she joined in the conversation, seeming to relax. Soon they docked at Old Harbor. By the time they reached The Roosting Place, the sky flamed in the west with deep ribbons of orange, melon, and coral. Keith would have liked to enjoy the sunset with Shae, or what he could see of it over the trees, but she dashed up the porch steps and into the inn before he could suggest it. Frustrated, Keith lingered on the porch and eyed the partially open door, wondering what he could say to fix things between them.

"Tiffany!"

At Shae's agonized shout, Keith rushed into the inn. No one was in the lobby, except Katie, who stood behind the desk, her eyes wide.

"Where's Shae?" he asked.

She pointed down the hallway that led to the old storage room. As he approached it, he saw the door standing ajar.

Inside, Tiffany stood on the second rung of the stepladder, her face a mask of shock. She stared down at Shae, who knelt beside the ladder and picked up something off the floor. On closer scrutiny, Keith could see it was the crystal angel that he'd tried to examine his first week at the inn.

"Oh, no!" Shae moaned.

"I'm sorry, Shae. I didn't mean to. I just wanted to look at it. And then when you came in here all mad, like you did, it slipped out of my hand. . . ." Tiffany's words trailed away as Shae's gaze snapped upward.

"It's chipped, Tiffany. The wing is chipped."

"I'm really sorry," the girl said in a voice trembling with tears. "I. . .I never meant to break it."

"You had no right to come in here without permission," Shae bit out, rising to her feet and cradling the angel.

Seeing that Tiffany was shaking all over, Keith strode into the room. "Shae, calm down. It was an accident."

Shae turned on him, her dark eyes full of pain and anger. "Stay out of it, Keith."

"She was my mother too!" Tiffany screeched, tears rolling down her face. "I may have been a little girl when she died, but I loved her just as much!" With a loud sob, she jumped down from the stepladder and made a beeline for the door.

Shae's eyes closed, and she took a shaky breath.

Keith moved toward her. "Are you okay?"

She looked his way. He was struck by the childlike vulnerability clouding her face. Moved with compassion, he reached out to touch her, but she drew back. "Really, I'm fine. I'm tired. It's just been a long day."

His gaze lowered to the angel she still cradled to her breast. "Want me to see if I can fix that? I used to be pretty handy with a glue gun."

She gave a little shake of her head, a faint troubled smile on her lips. "It's just a piece of glass, right? Don't worry about it. It's not that big a deal." Her words didn't mesh with the tone of her voice. She stepped around him. "I've got work to do before I turn in. Thanks for taking me to meet your family."

At the reminder, he grimaced. "I'm just sorry about what happened with Heather. I had no idea she would show—"

"Really, Keith. It's okay." She looked at him again. "I understand." With jerky steps she hurried out the door.

Keith noticed she didn't replace the angel on the shelf, but instead took it with her.

⁂

Huge celestial beings, their wings spanning across the sky, loomed over the little family who laughed and frolicked on the sandy beach not far from the lighthouse. Shae called out, but they couldn't seem to hear. As she watched, the angels' faces became grotesque, frightening. She screamed. But no sound issued from her mouth.

Her mother looked up and spotted her, smiling, motioning for her to join them. Shae seemed to be the only one capable of seeing the menacing angels overhead. She watched, horrified, as one of them took its mighty sword and struck her father down. Shae soundlessly screamed again and tried to run to

help. But her way was littered with shards of broken crystal—
her feet, barefoot and bleeding. She looked up and helplessly
watched as the angel struck her mother down from behind. . .

"Shae!"

Insistent hands shook her. Her eyes flickered open, but the
room was dark and she couldn't see well. Her heart banged
against her rib cage. Her throat felt raw and raspy. The fra-
grance of spicy cologne filled her nostrils.

"Keith?" she whispered.

"It's me. You were having a nightmare."

Remembering, she shuddered and held to his arms.

"Are you okay?" he asked gently.

"I. . .I think so." With his help, she inched up to a sitting
position against the pillow and noticed she lay on the couch
in the family parlor. To her left, snow filled the TV screen
with soft static. "It was the dream again."

She stiffened. Why had she told him that?

He sank to the edge of the cushion, near her legs. The blue-
white glow from the television made it easy to see the concern written in his eyes. "Do you want to tell me about it?"

For a moment she considered, then shook her head. She'd
never told anyone about the nightmare. "It was just a silly
dream."

"Not silly enough to keep you from screaming out."

Her eyes widened. "I screamed?"

He nodded. "Several times. If I hadn't been walking by the
door, I wouldn't have heard you. You had it closed."

Embarrassed, Shae dropped her gaze to the blanket. She
crossed her arms over her sweatshirt, hugging herself.

"I'm a good listener," Keith said softly. "Sometimes it helps
to talk."

Shae gave a short nod. She felt drained, helpless. What was
left of her defenses began to crumble under his gentle concern,
his strength, and his protection. He knew the worst and hadn't
ridiculed her or run away—though he didn't know the details.
She'd never told a soul any of it—not even her grandmother.

For over seven intolerable years she'd carried the burden alone. . . .

"Please, Shae, let me help," he said, putting a light hand on the blanket that covered her upraised knee. "Don't shut me out. I care."

At his soft plea, she closed her eyes and nodded. Before she could change her mind, the whole horrible dream spilled from her mouth. Afterward he took her in his arms and held her head close to his chest for a long time. The reassuring steady thud of his heartbeat calmed her trembling.

"It was just a dream," he murmured, smoothing a hand over her hair. "Just a dream."

Shae closed her eyes. It was much more than that. It was her penance. Something she deserved. But for him to understand, she would have to tell him what happened that day. . .and suddenly, she wanted to, though she didn't understand why.

Her gaze went to the crystal figurine on the coffee table. Light from the TV sparked off its gown and wings. She shuddered.

"Shae?" Keith asked, worried.

She took a shaky breath. Lying with her head against his chest like this, one of his arms wrapped around her back, his hand stroking her hair, made it easier. Much easier than facing him.

"I. . .I've had the dream since the accident," she began, her voice a raspy whisper, "since after the picnic at the bluffs. I was a little older than Tiffany at the time." She took an unsteady breath. "I had turned into a rebel. My parents weren't around much, and I was angry. I took up with the wrong crowd and got into drinking and partying. We three kids stayed here with Grandma that summer, and when my parents suddenly showed up one week we were thrilled. I had thought we'd go home with them when they left—that they'd come to get us."

Shae swallowed hard. "At the picnic they told us they were off to Europe in the morning and that we were to stay behind.

I got really mad, screamed a lot of things—things I didn't really mean." She felt the tears burn her nose. "I yelled that I wished they were dead. That they only cared about their career, and that if they really cared about us they would take another flight and stay longer than just three days. Then I ran from the beach and up the stairs to the road. A friend of mine was driving by. I hitched a ride with her, and she lit up a joint to calm me down."

Keith's arm tightened around Shae's trembling back, giving her the courage she needed to go on.

"When I got to the inn, I couldn't think straight I was so high. I'd told my friend what happened, and she supported me—making me even angrier with my parents. I ran to my room. On my bureau was a crystal angel Mama had given me—a twin to the one Tiffany broke. Mama told me when she gave it to me that it was a reminder—that whenever we were apart, each of us would have the angel to remind us God and His angels were watching over us—holding our family together. I picked it up and hurled it at the wall. I–It shattered. Later Mama came to talk to me, but I w–wouldn't listen, and we got into a fight."

Shae sobbed brokenly, putting a hand to her face. "Th–they changed their plans to s–spend more time with me. Their plane crashed—and they died."

Keith stilled his hand on her hair and cupped her head. "Oh, Shae, I'm sorry. So very sorry. . ."

"If it h–hadn't been for me, they would've taken that earlier flight. They'd s–still be alive today. It's my fault they're dead."

"Shae, that's not true."

"Yes, it is. I killed them."

Shae's soft, pitiful words threatened to rip his heart. He pulled away from her and cradled her tear-smudged face, lifting it to see into her eyes. "You did not kill them, Shae. What happened was an accident, something over which you had no control. It's understandable that you wanted more time with them—and most children have tantrums and say and do things they don't mean. You can't go on blaming yourself for what happened. It's not your fault."

She didn't answer, only looked at him with those dark, wounded eyes. Keith could see that she didn't believe a word he said. Drawing her close again, he closed his eyes, searching for something to say to convince her. But this went too deep for him. She needed more help than he could give.

Hoping God would still listen to him, despite all he'd done, Keith sent a silent prayer upward for Shae.

❧

Shae riffled the corner pages of the ledger and stared out the window, thinking. Last night, when she confided in Keith after the horrible nightmare, she'd temporarily forgotten the upsetting incident with Heather. Since then, she'd mulled it over. Remembering Keith's chagrined explanations in the car on the way back to Port Judith then reflecting on how Heather had approached Shae—immediately making it a point to imply that she and Keith had something going—Shae was more inclined to believe Keith innocent. Or was she just so naïve concerning men that she didn't know better?

The rapid click of high heels startled her, and she turned her head and watched as Hillary rushed through the open door. One look at her anxious expression told Shae it was going to be a bad day.

"Shae, I don't know what to do. Robert didn't come home last night. I called his friends and found out he went to the mainland again. And I don't know what he does there, or who to contact to get ahold of him."

Alarm prickled through Shae. "I'm sure he'll be back soon."

"When he's gone there before, he's usually back before morning," Hillary worriedly continued, as though she hadn't heard. "And it's four o'clock now."

Shae's eyes flew to the clock. Four o'clock! She'd have to get on the phone fast if she were to find a replacement for tonight's floor show. "Hillary, go home. He may be trying to call. I'll find someone else. But, Hillary," her voice held gentle warning, "this can't continue. Please explain it to Robert when you talk to him. I have an inn to run."

Hillary nodded, tears swimming in her eyes. Shae rose from behind her desk and went to her, giving the distraught woman a hug. "It'll be okay. There's probably a simple explanation for everything."

After Hillary left, Shae set to work. Fifteen minutes later she folded her arms on top of her desk and laid her head down on them, too discouraged to go on.

"That bad, huh?"

Hearing Keith's warm baritone, Shae lifted her head and gave a dry laugh. "Hillary can't perform tonight—Robert's missing. And unless I hire fifteen-year-old Phillip Starnes with his amazing tuba, or Billy Grafton and his dancing dog, Fluffy, then I haven't got an act."

"So I take it that means you'll have to provide the entertainment tonight."

She gave a weary nod, her eyes going to the crystal angel now sitting on her desk. "I'm just not sure I can sing after last night."

A long pause. "Would you like some help?"

Surprised, Shae looked at him. "Help?"

"I'll sing with you. We'll make it a duet."

Her eyes widened. "Aren't you afraid your cover will be blown? That you'll be recognized and stampeded?"

"No," he said calmly. "From what I've seen, the audience that frequents your nightclub is mostly of an older generation. I think I'll be safe. Besides, none of the tourists that have stayed here seemed to recognize me."

"Well, that's true," she said uncertainly. "But won't Freddie mind?"

"He's in his room with his laptop, answering E-mail and making calls. He won't know. Besides, he doesn't *own* me, Shae. I don't have to get his permission."

Mulling his clipped words over, she rubbed her temples.

"Headache?" he asked more softly.

She nodded. "Not a bad one. Just started an hour ago."

"Why don't you go upstairs, lie down, and I'll bring you some tea. I've heard chamomile is great when you need to relax."

Despite the constant dull thudding at her temples, Shae managed a smile. "I appreciate the offer, Keith, but there just isn't time. The show starts in less than three hours. I'll pop a couple of aspirin or something." She considered his other offer. Remembering how supportive he'd been last night, and how comforting his support had felt, Shae regarded him. "But I would like you to sing with me."

His eyes lit up. "I look forward to it."

≈

Not long before show time, Keith searched for Shae but couldn't find her. He approached Katie at the desk. "Have you seen Shae?"

"In the kitchen, I think."

Keith thanked her and headed that way. He found Shae standing by the sink, tossing a half-squeezed lemon into the disposal.

"What are you doing?"

She held up a glass full of something that looked like milky water. "Lemon water. It helps clear my throat, so I can sing better. Want some?"

Keith stared doubtfully at the concoction. "Er, no thanks." He pulled a small aerosol spray bottle from his pocket. "I use this—it's specially designed for singers."

She lifted the glass in a toast. "Oh. Well, bottoms up."

Wondering how she could stand to chug such sour stuff, he took another look at her deep blue, sequined cocktail dress. "Sorry. All I have to wear is this," he said, motioning to his blue cotton shirt and gray pants. "I didn't exactly come prepared."

She pulled the empty glass away from her mouth and set it on the counter. "No problem. At least we match. That's what's important." Her brow furrowed. "And of course it's important that our voices blend well. I hadn't thought of that when I agreed to this. What if we don't click?"

Keith smiled. "Well, if you're ready, let's go find out."

They went to the dining room and hurried backstage. Shae suddenly whirled to face him, as if something had just occurred to her. "Keith, do you know any show tunes from the golden years of music? That's basically what we sing here, though we do one or two modern songs too." She named a few of the more modern ones.

Keith shook his head. "Don't know any of them. Sorry."

"Hmm." Averting her gaze, Shae screwed her mouth up in a thoughtful expression. She snapped her fingers, looking up. "What about 'You Light Up My Life'? Know that one?"

"I remember my mom listening to it when I was a kid." Keith frowned. "Not sure I know the words, though."

Shae hurried to a table against the wall that held a receptacle of sheet music. Thumbing through the large box, she grinned, triumphantly pulling a paper out. "There. Think you could learn the words in the time before we go on?"

"I've been in trickier situations." He took the music. "But are we only going to sing one song, or do a set?"

Shae stuck out her lower lip, blowing out a loud breath that stirred her hair at her temple. "I hadn't thought of that. I'm usually so much better prepared. . . ."

"Want me to sing one or two of my songs?"

She gave him a faint smile. "No offense, Keith. But they rock a bit too much for this place."

"I could do 'The Old Rugged Cross,' " he joked.

She shook her head, then stared, her brow slowly wrinkling in thought. "You know, that might not be such a bad idea."

"Here?" Keith said incredulously. "In a nightclub?"

"I own the place, remember? And what the manager says, goes." She grinned.

"Your customers might not like it."

She shrugged. "They're lucky to be getting any music at all—especially with how this day has gone. Besides, as you pointed out, our crowds are usually older. I say we give it a shot."

"Okay, if you're sure. And if we're doing something like that anyway, maybe for a third number we can sing 'Angels to Watch over Us.' Got the sheet music for that? It's a gospel song from about fifteen years ago, I think. It was a favorite of Mom's. I remember some of the words, but not all of them."

Shae stiffened and turned away. "No. Sorry." She pulled out another sheet and handed it over sideways without facing him. "How about this one?"

Keith studied her, not sure if he was just imagining Shae's sudden withdrawal, or if it was the stress of the moment. Probably it was the situation that made her shoulders tremble and her voice come out funny. Memory of her nightmare flashed through his mind, and he mentally kicked himself. Of course she wouldn't want to sing a song like that right now!

He slowly pulled her into a gentle hug. "Buck up, Partner," he whispered, "we can do this."

She nodded against his chest.

Thirty minutes later, they took the stage amid polite applause. No one announced them, and for that Keith was grateful. He'd been pretty certain he wouldn't be recognized when he'd first offered to sing with Shae, but it was still a relief that no face in the crowd lit with recognition. Although it was hard to see anyone in the dark area with the bright lights of the stage blinding him.

He and Shae had practiced backstage earlier, but here at the microphone, with Shae playing the piano and Keith sitting beside her, he was amazed at just how harmoniously their voices blended. Judging from the enthusiastic audience response, the crowd was pleased as well. They sang two more numbers, and afterward Keith took the piano to sing the gospel hymn, hoping Shae wasn't mistaken and it would be received well. After the last note trailed in the air, there were a few seconds of nerve-wracking silence, followed by a loud wave of applause. Keith let out a relieved breath, faced the crowd, and inclined his head in a bow while Shae did the same, also saying a soft "thank you" into the mike.

Once backstage, he pulled her into a tight hug, which she returned. "You did great," he said. "We belong together, Shae. Our voices blend so well—"

"Young man? Young man!" A plump middle-aged woman in a green suit dress waddled up to Keith, another woman with her. Wetness glimmered on the first woman's cheeks, and she smiled at him. "I just wanted to tell you how much your last song moved me. It was lovely. I haven't heard that song since my father sang it."

Keith smiled. "Thank you. I'm glad you enjoyed it."

"Do you sing? I mean professionally."

"Uh," Keith looked to Shae, "now and then."

"Well, you have a wonderful voice. God gave you a remarkable talent, and I hope you continue using it for Him."

Keith just stared, managed a nod.

She pulled a card from her clasped purse. "I'm Theda London. I'm a pastor's wife, and I would love for you to come sing at our church this summer—in Connecticut."

"I'm sorry. I'm leaving for California Friday. I'm only visiting Rhode Island."

"Oh, what a shame. Well, if you're ever in town. . ."

Keith thanked the woman again, and after she left, he turned to Shae. She looked up at him. "I didn't know you were leaving Friday."

Keith grimaced. "I was going to wait for a better time to tell you. There are several things I want to say—"

"Shae!"

At Hillary's frantic cry, they turned in her direction as she rushed toward them. A panic-stricken look filled her eyes. "I just heard. Robert is in the hospital—he. . .he had a car accident. He's in emergency surgery now. Oh, Shae, what am I going to do?"

"You're going to go to him." Shae looped an arm around Hillary. "And I'll go with you."

Hillary shook her head. "He's on the mainland, Shae. And the last ferry has left by now."

"I can try to charter a flight at the airport," Keith said.

"The airport?" Shae echoed hollowly.

"Thank you, Keith," Hillary sniffled. "I just can't seem to think straight. I don't know what to do." She turned teary eyes Shae's way. "You're the only friend I've got on the island. Will you come with me? I'm so scared."

Keith noticed how Shae's face had paled. He put a hand to the middle of her back. "I'll come too."

She stared at him, then slowly nodded, terror in her eyes.

ten

Shae tried to push down her panic as she stared at the small plane. The reverberations on the tarmac, coming from the loud engine, matched the pounding of her heart. How could she go through with this? She'd flown many times before, but not since her parents died. Twice she'd almost declined and returned to the inn, but each time Shae had glanced at Hillary's distraught face and kept silent. Yet Keith understood.

Shae looked his way now. He stared at her with sympathetic concern etched on his features and held out a hand. She took it, clutching it hard, desperately soaking up every ounce of support he offered. She was doubly relieved she had told him everything. Well, almost everything. There was no reason to tell him the rest. He would be gone in a few days.

Saddened by the thought, Shae wrinkled her brow.

"Watch your step," the pilot warned when Shae slipped on the stair leading up to the metal monster that she was willfully allowing to devour her. . . .

"I'm right behind you," Keith said close to her ear, helping her into the plane.

The takeoff was bumpy, and Shae gripped Keith's arm with both hands, feeling her heart lurch. Unable to stop herself, she took one brief look out the small window at the dark ocean below—too far below for her peace of mind. The same ocean that had sucked her parents into its great belly.

Shae's eyelids slammed shut. She wouldn't look. Her fingernails made creases in Keith's jacket. Somehow, she had to find the strength to be there for Hillary—but she couldn't think about anything like that now, when she felt so weak inside.

Keith had said the trip to the mainland only took a little over ten minutes, but it seemed more like eons to Shae. When the plane finally set down with a powerful jolt, shaking her in her seat as if it would try to destroy her yet, her eyes flew open. She watched with horrified fascination as they sped down the runway. When they came to a stop and deplaned, her legs trembled so badly she found it difficult to walk, and again Keith stayed beside her, this time putting an arm around her waist until she'd regained some composure.

"I'm proud of you," he said for her ears alone. "I know that wasn't easy."

Shae nodded, gave him a faint smile then looked at Hillary. Now that she'd safely made it through the ordeal, Shae needed to focus on her friend. "You okay, Hillary?"

The woman gave a slight nod, staring at the ground. "They wouldn't tell me much," she murmured. Frightened eyes turned Shae's way. "Oh, Shae. What if he doesn't make it? What will I do without him?"

Shae moved from Keith and put an arm around Hillary's shoulders. "Let's not think about things like that right now. I'm with you, and I'll stay tonight as long as you need me."

After a long taxi ride, they arrived at the hospital. Coming out of the dark night into the glaring lights of the pristine building temporarily blinded Shae. Keith, as he usually did when in public, slipped on his sunglasses, and for a moment Shae wished she also had a pair. The events of the past few hours had brought on her headache again. At least she'd had the foresight to exchange the scratchy sequined dress for a comfortable sweatshirt and pants before leaving the inn. They approached the information desk, where a harried nurse glanced up.

"I'm Mrs. Collins," Hillary said, a tremor in her voice. "I was told my husband is in surgery. He. . .he had an accident."

The nurse directed them to the small waiting area outside surgery. Hillary sank onto one of the cushioned chairs while Shae informed the nurse behind the computer at the nurses' station that Mrs. Collins had arrived, and asked if there was any news. The nurse shook her head.

Keith went to a nearby table where an automatic coffee-maker sat and poured three cups of hot coffee. He handed Hillary a cup, and she took it with a soft "thank you."

The minute hand on the big face of the round clock above the nurses' counter seemed to creep by as though taking its last breath. Except for their presence, the waiting area was clear. Nurses hurried about their duties, their white shoes creaking softly down immaculate corridors. From beyond the nurses' station, the muted ding-ding of a bell issued a quiet alert.

Keith thumbed through a magazine. Hillary sat forward and stared into space, ignoring her coffee, and Shae sat quietly beside her, glancing at her watch now and then to be sure the clock was right.

"What's taking so long?" Hillary moaned. "It's been over two hours since I got the phone call."

Shae put an arm around her shoulders, not knowing what to say. After the minute hand had crept halfway to the other side of the round clock, a tall man in scrubs appeared in the corridor. His face was lined and weary as he approached. "Mrs. Collins?"

Hillary stood, her face blanched by fear, and went to meet him, Shae by her side. "I'm Mrs. Collins."

His brown eyes were solemn. "I'm Dr. Brent. Your husband is being transferred to recovery. He's a lucky man, Mrs. Collins. His heart stopped once on the operating table, but we were able to resuscitate him. We stopped the internal bleeding, but the next few hours are crucial. As for his facial. . ." He broke off, obviously ill at ease when he noted how Hillary folded against Shae. "The lacerations were extensive and will require plastic surgery at a later date—"

"P–plastic surgery," Hillary repeated.

"Yes," he said more gently. "I won't lie to you—his chances of making it are slim, but we're doing everything we can. And Mrs. Collins, if you believe in prayer, I'd recommend it. If your husband does pull through, it's going to be a long haul on the road ahead."

"Wh—when can I see him?" she breathed.

"As soon as he has been moved to the ICU," the doctor promised. After a few more words describing Robert's other injuries, he left them, promising to keep her informed.

Shae held onto Hillary, who went limp against her. "Let's sit down," she suggested softly, steering her back to the chair and taking a place beside her. "Is there any family that should be notified?"

Hillary shook her head. "Robert is a foster child, and never talked about his family." Her voice came dull. "My parents live in Portsmouth, but I doubt they'd care. They never did like Robert."

"Still you should call them," Shae said, putting a gentle hand to her back. "I'm sure they care about you and would want to be here for you." In Shae's opinion, Hillary needed something to do, to occupy her mind. Such things helped when the grief was overwhelming.

Hillary nodded and walked woodenly to the phone on a nearby table. Keith took the empty chair next to Shae. "I heard the doctor from here. He has the type of voice that carries. How's she doing?"

"Not good. About as well as can be expected." Shae put her hands to her temples and rubbed with circular motions.

"Headache back?"

She nodded.

"Let me."

Shae was surprised when she felt his hand slip under her hair and circle the nape of her neck, his fingers beginning a slow, firm massage. She closed her eyes and relaxed.

"You've been under a lot of stress. You need rest. Have you eaten today?"

Shae thought back. Had she? "Breakfast. I had breakfast."

"As soon as they allow Hillary to see her husband, we're going to the cafeteria to get you some food."

"I can't leave her now," Shae protested.

"If you don't take care of yourself, you won't be any good

for your friend. Especially if they have to put you in one of those hospital beds."

Shae gave a reluctant nod.

Later, after a nurse finally informed Hillary that she could see Robert, Shae told Hillary she'd be back soon and walked with Keith to the elevator. Inside the small enclosure, two young girls stopped chattering and eyed Keith. They began to whisper to one another, and Shae caught a few of their words.

"Is it him?

"I don't know—ask him."

"Me! Why don't you?"

When the elevator doors whooshed open, Keith hurried out with Shae, turned the corner, and ducked into a gift shop, behind a tall revolving book rack. "That was close," he breathed.

"Maybe it's not safe for you to be here," Shae said. "I've witnessed firsthand how girls react when they find out who you are—well, let's just say a hospital isn't a place for that to happen."

Keith let out a harsh breath. "You're right."

"Excuse me, Sir," a woman's voice said from behind the counter. "We're closing now."

Keith nodded, scanning the aisles. He grabbed a blue bandanna from a rack and laid it on the counter. "Do I still have time to buy this?"

The woman nodded and rang up his purchase. Shae wondered, but didn't question, her gaze going to a nearby shelf of magazines. On the cover of one, Keith's face smiled at her. She strode across the carpet to get a better look. Curious, she pulled the publication out and read the caption beside it: *Pop Rock Star Offers Himself As Dream Date. Who Will Be The Lucky Girl?*

Sudden heat rushing to her face, Shae curiously flipped through the pages until she found the four-page full-color section on Keith. She skimmed the article, frowning.

"Don't believe everything you read," Keith's low voice

suddenly came from behind her, near her ear. "I've heard he's really an okay kinda guy."

Startled, Shae jumped and dropped the magazine, another wave of heat flooding her face. Hastily, she bent and plucked it up from the floor, stuffing it back in its slot. She turned, her gaze going to the glass door.

"Will you help me tie this?"

She looked at him then. Keith wore the bandanna over his head, biker style, and was trying to knot it in the back.

"Sure." She stepped around him and tied the scarf, tucking his blond hair underneath so it wouldn't show.

"Shae," he muttered, "seriously—about that magazine spread. . .a lot of things are often blown out of proportion for publicity's sake. . . ."

She forced her tone to be light, though she was still a little embarrassed at being caught poring over an article concerning him. "Oh. So you really weren't a wild playboy who liked to party every night and date a different woman every month?"

Keith groaned. "Okay, the first few years in the business I was a jerk and a snob. I'll be the first to admit it. But I don't play fast anymore. I got tired of that lifestyle—"

"Hey, I was just teasing. Don't worry about it. And concerning what you said about publicity—believe me, I understand." She gave a pat to the head covering. "There. All finished."

He turned. "How do I look?"

Grinning, she cocked her brow. "You really want to know? A couple of gold hoops in each ear, and maybe some tattoos to add to the outfit of that bandanna and your sunglasses and leather jacket—and you won't have to worry about anyone chasing after you, Keith. Except maybe to throw you out." She chuckled. "You look like a highly suspicious character."

"Thanks," he said drolly. "But if it shields my identity, then so be it. Let's get out of here."

After a quick bite at the cafeteria, Keith and Shae returned to the waiting area where Hillary sat, staring at the curtains. Her face was set in a frozen mask, and she twisted her wedding ring on her finger.

"Hillary?"

The blond turned her way, her eyes hurt and angry. "I found out he had a woman with him, Shae. He'd been drinking. He broke through a guardrail and sent the car hurtling down the embankment. He flew through the windshield—wasn't wearing his seat belt. The woman is in critical condition."

"Oh, Hillary," Shae breathed, sinking to the chair beside her, not knowing what to say.

Hillary gave a short laugh that sounded more like a sob. Her gaze drifted to her hand again. "If he survives, he's in a lot of trouble with the law."

Shae put the sack with the croissant she'd brought for Hillary on the lamp table next to her, knowing food would be the furthest thing from her mind. Sitting beside her, Shae put an arm around her friend. Sometimes quiet support was best.

❧

After an uncomfortable night sprawled upright in a chair, sleeping with the back of his neck against its hard rim, Keith opened his eyes. He was relieved for the comfort of his sunglasses, which helped dim the bright light coming through a slit in the curtain. The next thing he noticed was that Shae was missing. She'd slept with her head against his shoulder almost all night, and though that part of him was stiff, Keith didn't really mind. He'd go through it again, to have her beside him.

Shae Stevens was a very special woman, different from anyone he'd ever known. Now he had more than one reason for visiting Rhode Island on a regular basis. He only hoped that she was in favor of the idea. She still seemed as though she were holding a part of herself back from him, and he wanted to know everything concerning her. At first his desire had stemmed from curiosity, then the need to help her in whatever way he could as a friend, but now he knew his feelings went deeper than any of those reasons. He was in love.

Keith uncurled from his position and straightened his

cramped body, spotting Hillary across from him, riffling
through a magazine.

"How's your husband?"

She looked up. "The same. He's still in ICU. There's been
no change in his condition."

"Sorry to hear that." Keith hunched his shoulders then brought
them down, trying to get out the kinks. "Where's Shae?"

"She ran into an old friend in the rest room this morning. Her
mother had surgery a few days ago. Shae went to visit her."

Keith nodded and stood. "I'll be back. I need to stretch
my legs."

He left the ICU waiting room, where they'd relocated in the
middle of the night, and strode the hospital corridors. While he
roamed the area, he thought about Shae, ignoring the wide-
eyed looks cast in his direction. Curious, he studied his reflection in a dark office window as he walked past, stopped, and
took off his sunglasses so he could see more clearly. The bandanna had inched up and blond hair snaked out over his collar.
Giving a disgusted snort, he started to tuck it back in.

Three teenagers came around the corridor, one of them carrying a basket of flowers. They slowed their steps as their eyes
turned his way, and they began to whisper to one another. One
of them bravely piped up, "Aren't you Keith Travers?"

"No comprende," he answered hurriedly, wondering why
they weren't in school. He slipped his shades back on, ducked
into a nearby elevator, and took it to the next floor. As he walked
the spotless corridors, he noticed most of the room doors were
open wide, for any visitors that happened by, he supposed.

Hands in his jacket pockets, Keith wondered about the
future and if he should renew his contract. His mind again
went to what that pastor's wife had told him the night before,
about how he should use his voice for God. Her words
exactly echoed what his granny had told him many years ago,
stunning Keith. Was God trying to get his attention? But why
would He after all Keith had done?

He turned the corner into another corridor, startled to hear soft singing coming from a nearby room. Lifting the bandanna off one ear to try to hear more clearly, he was even more surprised to discover the voice belonged to Shae. In dazed curiosity, he halted beside the entrance of a patient's room and leaned his shoulder against the wall.

That tune. . .he knew it. He'd heard it before. And then it hit him. It was the song he'd suggested they sing last night, the song Shae had said she didn't have the music to.

From the way her voice shook, Keith could tell it was a struggle for her to sing. After the last sweet note trembled in the air, an elderly woman's frail voice floated into the corridor. "Thank you, Marcia. Thank you for giving a dying old woman one last request. Your mother and father. . .they would've been proud. You've done credit to their name. . . ."

Keith wrinkled his brow. *Marcia?* He puzzled over the woman's strange words, at the same time recalling everything he'd learned about Shae these past weeks. Her parents' tragic death. . .her nightmares and guilt. . .her hesitancy to talk about herself. . .Marcia. Marcia Stevens.

The truth hit with a powerful blow. Keith turned his back to the wall, leaning against it, and closed his eyes in shock.

At last, he'd found the missing piece of the puzzle.

৶

Shae overtly studied Keith across the table in the hospital cafeteria. When she'd left Mrs. Braxton and had returned to Hillary with the intent to take her friend to breakfast and force food down her throat if she had to, Shae noticed Keith's strange behavior. When she'd suggested they go to the cafeteria, he looked at her as if he'd never seen her before.

Since being here, he'd seemed distant, unfocused, hardly speaking a word to either of them. For the extroverted Keith, that was tantamount to a world crisis. Even Hillary seemed to notice his preoccupied behavior as he toyed with his food, for she gave him a puzzled glance, then looked at Shae with lifted brows.

Shae shrugged her shoulders at her friend's silent inquiry.

She had no idea what was bothering him.

Picking up a forkful of sausage, she stuck it in her mouth and chewed. She tried to make it go down past the lump in her throat, but she may as well have been eating putty for all the taste she got out of it. Pushing her plate away, she noted with relief that Hillary had managed to eat, though nowhere near her normal appetite. Shae took a sip of juice. It helped ease the lump, but not much. At least the headache wasn't as bad as last night. She glanced at her watch.

"Hillary, I hate to leave you, but I have to get back to the inn, and the ferry will be leaving soon." She blotted her mouth with a napkin. "I really wish there was someone who could be here for you until your mom gets here. . . ."

Hillary gave a weak smile. "I'll be fine."

Shae rose to give the blond a hug. "Call me with any news?"

Hillary nodded. "Thank you, Shae. You've been a true friend."

Shae looked at Keith, who was staring at her with a slight frown. She wished she could see his eyes behind the shades. Maybe then she could determine just what he was thinking. "Ready?"

He nodded, and after another quick good-bye to Hillary, Shae walked with him to the front where they called a taxi.

Once in the back of the cab, which smelled of old vinyl and grease, Keith removed his sunglasses, closed his eyes, and rubbed the bridge of his nose. When several minutes elapsed with only silence between them, Shae looked at him uneasily. "Is something bothering you, Keith? You've been acting strange all morning."

He turned to her, his blue eyes steady. "Were you ever planning to tell me who you really are?" His voice came out low, almost sad.

"What. . .what do you mean?" Her heart began beating a mile a minute.

"Marcia, I know."

Feeling the world cave in, she closed her eyes.

eleven

"How did you find out?" Shae asked, her voice hoarse, panicked.

Keith watched in concern as her face went a shade pale. Maybe he shouldn't have spoken; maybe that had been a mistake. Yet, since leaving his post by her friend's hospital door, Keith had been able to think of little else but the discovery he had happened on.

"Pure chance. I was walking through the hospital and heard you sing to your friend." He fiddled with the temples of his sunglasses. "What I don't understand is why the big secret?"

Shae let out a humorless laugh. "You shouldn't have to ask that, Keith, knowing what you know about me. Knowing that I'm responsible for my parents' deaths—for robbing the world of two of the most popular gospel singers of the decade."

He shook his head. "It wasn't your fault. You can't predict the future, Shae, you couldn't have known what would happen."

Seeing the cabdriver frequently peer into the rearview mirror, Keith grimaced his way. "Do you mind?"

The cabbie looked back out the windshield.

"Nothing you say can ever convince me of that," Shae replied quietly, staring at the back of the seat in front of her. "I've lived with the pain and guilt for over seven long years. What makes you think I can let go of it now?"

Her gaze swung his way. "You ask why I protected my anonymity? Why the big secret? Well, I'll tell you. It's because I didn't want the reporters to find out who I am. As I'm sure you know, they can be very sneaky about getting you to say things you don't mean, things you don't want the public to know." Angry tears shone in her eyes. "You would have made

129

a great reporter, Keith. You've found out more about me in three weeks than most people who've known me my whole life."

"Shae. . ."

"And now let me anticipate your next question, for I'm sure you have one," she interrupted, her voice growing a little hysterical and raising a notch. "Why wouldn't I want the public to know? Because I would've never been able to stand the hate or revulsion or anger or pity in people's eyes if they somehow found out that it was because of me that Trey and Marilyn Stevens' plane got caught in a bad storm and crashed in the middle of the Atlantic Ocean."

The taxi swerved, the cabbie's wide eyes flashing to the rearview mirror again.

"I think we'd better have this conversation elsewhere," Keith muttered, noticing they had neared the docks. "Pull over here," he told the cabdriver.

After paying the cabbie, Keith led Shae to a nearby bench.

"We'll miss the ferry," she mumbled.

"No, we won't. It won't be here for another twenty minutes, and the dock is about a five-minute walk from here. And anyway, if we do miss it, we can always take the next one."

Shae didn't say a word, just slumped onto the bench like a marionette whose strings had been cut loose. She stared at the ground, frowning. Keith heaved a quiet breath of frustration, and sank beside her.

"I wish I knew what to say to convince you you're wrong about all this, Shae, but I don't seem to have the words."

She gave a humorless little sound, bordering on a laugh. "Well, that's a first!"

Wondering how he could reach her and make her see the truth, Keith studied her profile. Her long hair hung like a black silk drape, covering part of her jaw. Her eyes were downcast, hands stuffed into the pockets of her sweatshirt.

This sullen woman was far removed from the bright-faced child with the braids and braces who sang every year on her parents' annual Christmas television specials. Now that Keith thought about it, a boy had been on there too—Tommy, probably—but the show had mainly focused on Shae and her parents. Keith remembered lying on his stomach on the floor in front of the television, his chin propped in his hands, and watching the specials with the rest of his family. After one of Shae's solos, his mom would go on and on about what a lovely voice the Stevens' little girl had, and how she would probably be as famous as her parents someday. But at the time, Keith had done what most typical adolescent boys would do. Just shrugged it off, uninterested.

But now he was interested. Very interested. *Oh, God, how can I help her?* he thought in frustration.

It's not your place to do that, Son. Direct her to Me.

Keith blinked when the gentle and unexpected words filtered through his mind. Shock that God would still want to use Keith—much less talk to him after all he'd willfully done wrong—brought emotion to Keith's throat that he awkwardly swallowed down. And with it came the vivid realization that God had never turned His back on Keith, even when Keith had been at his worst. But rather, Keith had turned his back on God. God was just waiting for Keith's return, like the father of the prodigal, like Keith's earthly father had done. Waiting and hoping. . .

"Shae," Keith began, a slight tremor to his voice, "forgive me for being a hypocrite."

She turned and looked at him then, her face full of wary surprise. "What do you mean?"

"All this time I've been trying to help you with your problems, trying to get you to see the truth—and failing badly at it, too, I might add—when I've been just as blind about my own problems. I've been running from the truth, just like you—unable and maybe a little afraid to accept it." He sighed. "And I seem to remember reading something in the Bible, a long time ago, about a blind man unable to lead a blind man because they'd both fall into a ditch."

She shook her head in obvious confusion. "I don't get what you're saying."

"What I'm saying is that I think you need to talk to someone about your fears. But I also think that person should be someone more qualified to do it. Like Pastor Williams."

Shae stared a moment then gave a short nod. "To tell the truth, I'd thought about it once or twice. Especially since I know that his profession binds him under a confidentiality type clause and that he wouldn't relate anything I told him to anyone else." She bit her upper lip. "But like I said, Keith, before you came along, I hadn't told anyone any of it. I just couldn't. Not even Grandma. Not even Tommy."

"But now that you've told one person—me—maybe it won't be as hard to open up a second time and talk to your pastor."

"Maybe." She grew thoughtful again. "Keith," she said looking down nervously, "please don't tell anyone what you've learned. About who I am, I mean. Some of Grandma's old friends know, of course, but there aren't many of them left on the island. I'd just rather no one knew the truth."

"I understand, and I hope you know I'd never do anything to hurt you. Though I may not agree with you in this, I'll keep your secret. You can trust me."

"Thanks," Shae said very softly, still not looking at him. She glanced at her watch. "I think we'd better make tracks for the ferry."

"Yeah, I guess so."

They rose from the bench and began walking to the spot where the ferry would dock. "Keith?"

"Yeah?" He sent a glance her way.

"About the other night, when I had the nightmare. I just want you to know that your being there with me helped a lot." She turned her head and gave a glimmer of a smile. "So you see, you didn't fail in everything concerning me."

"Thank you for telling me that, Shae."

Her admission meant more to him than she could know. It meant that she was opening up to him—a deliberate action on

her part, without her being coerced into it. Smiling, he held
his hand out to her, and she took it.

ð

Shae hung up the phone and frowned. Robert was still in
ICU. Hillary was holding up well under the circumstances,
and Shae was glad Hillary's mother was there to support her
daughter through this crisis. Tears had been in Hillary's voice
when she'd told Shae that her mother had said she'd been
praying for Hillary and Robert for the past few months now.
Maybe God would somehow work in their lives and bring
them to a turning point through this accident.

Turning point. Shae sighed. She had also reached a turning
point of sorts, now that Keith knew everything about her.
Speaking the truth aloud had forced her to dwell on the past
more often than she cared to. Yet it made her realize that she
did need some kind of help from somewhere if she was going
to successfully live in the present. . . .

"Hey, Shae," Tiffany said, breezing into the office. "So,
what are you wearing?"

Puzzled, Shae cast a fleeting look at her cream-colored cotton skirt and white blouse. "The same kind of thing I usually
wear when I'm working."

Tiffany rolled her eyes. "You can be so dense sometimes.
I'm talking about for the date tomorrow. You know, the one
with Keith."

Shae froze. *The date!* With all the turmoil that had rocked
her world this past week, the dream date coming up so soon
had completely slipped her mind. Her gaze went to the pile of
unanswered correspondence, bills, and the like. She'd taken
too much time away from work as it was, and tomorrow she'd
be gone all day with Keith. "Oh, I don't know. Probably a
pair of jeans and a sweatshirt I guess."

Tiffany gaped in horror. "You have got to be kidding. This
is Keith Travers we're talking about, Shae. Not some average
guy down the street. And remember, your picture is going to
be in a national magazine! You can't just go looking like

you're out for a jog or something."

Shae released an irritated sigh. "Well then, what do you suggest?"

Tiffany pondered. "Something romantic, but casual. Something you can dress up if you had to—that is, if you're going anywhere fancy."

Shae thought over her words. She and Keith had decided they would do a little of what both liked on their date. First, because of Shae's love of antiques and historic houses, they would visit The Breakers in Newport. Freddie had made special arrangements for a private morning tour. Then they would lunch at a dockside restaurant, window-shop at Old Harbor, and afterward charter a boat and go fishing. The evening would conclude with a romantic dinner by sunset. Or as romantic as you could get with a photographer and reporter breathing down your neck and eyeing your every move, telling you just how to pose and do things. Shae still remembered those days.

She studied her sister's excited features, relieved that they were talking again. Since the incident with the crystal angel, Tiffany had steered clear of her older sister, and Shae had never brought up that night, just wanting to forget about it.

Rising from the desk, deciding the work could wait, Shae smiled. "Okay, Tiff. What say you and I go raid my closet?"

"Cool." Tiffany beamed her a smile and walked upstairs with Shae.

Fifteen minutes later, Shae sighed, throwing the hanger with the ivory, lace-edged casual dress onto the fast-growing pile on her bed. "Okay, so what's wrong with this one?"

"It's just blah." Tiffany scoured through Shae's closet, sliding clothes down the rack with a sense of purpose. "Besides, the material is all wrong. You'll need something that won't get ruined by salt spray. And, Shae, that color is just not you."

Crossing her arms at her sister's emphatic statement, Shae arched an eyebrow. "So just when did you become Miss Fashion Wardrobe Consultant?"

Tiffany shrugged. "I've always been interested in clothes, you know that." She paused. "I've even thought about designing them—when I'm older anyway." Suddenly she beamed and pulled something from the rack. "Perfect! And underneath you can wear knee-length pants for the fishing thing if you want."

Shae eyed the rose-red durable blouse with the breast pockets and the black cotton skirt with small rose swirls on it. "I don't know, Tiffany. Short sleeves? I get cold really easily."

Tiffany scrunched her brow in thought. "Wear Mama's black lace shawl that Daddy bought for her—the one with the silver threads. I think I saw it in Grandma's closet."

"Mama's shawl?" Shae's voice came out hoarse.

Tiffany's gaze dropped to the floor. "Oh, yeah, that's right. You don't want to have anything to do with them anymore. It was just a suggestion," she mumbled.

Dismayed, Shae studied her sister. "Is that what you think? That I don't want to have anything to do with Mama and Daddy?"

"Well, sure. Why else would you want our identity kept such a secret? Liz said—" Tiffany clapped a hand over her mouth.

"Some secret," Shae said wryly, feeling a trace of panic.

"Oh, Liz won't tell—honest! She was too young to remember them, and I don't think her parents listened to gospel music anyway. So it's no big deal to her. Besides, she's known for years."

Shae nodded vaguely. "But it is a big deal to you, isn't it, Tiff?"

"Sure." Tiffany eyed her as though she couldn't believe Shae would ask such a dumb question. "Even though I was only seven when they died and don't remember as much about them as you or Tommy, I loved them too, Shae. And I want people to know who my parents were. I'm tired of hiding it. Tommy doesn't hide it."

Shae averted her gaze to the pile of clothes on the bed.

In a sudden, very grown-up gesture, Tiffany went to her

and gave her a one-armed hug. "Please don't be sad that I'm going to go live with them. I'll still come and visit."

Shae offered her a weak smile. "You're really looking forward to going, aren't you?"

"Well, sure. I mean Tommy's got a stable full of horses and everything. And you know how I like horses. And, well, then I can be myself. I won't have to worry about slipping up, or hiding who I am anymore because of who my parents were. And it will be really cool when the baby comes. It's so awesome that I'm going to be an aunt—and that I can help Linda with the baby and all."

"But what about Liz? I thought you two were close."

"She's coming to visit in August. Tommy said she could, and her parents already said okay."

"Poor Tommy," Shae said, her smile growing. "I wonder if he has any idea what he's in for."

Tiffany grinned. "Then you're okay with it? About me going?"

"I won't lie to you, Tiff. It hurts to see you go. I've never been separated from you, so this is going to be hard on me. Things certainly won't be the same around here once you're gone. But I want what's best for all concerned." She ruffled Tiffany's hair, which was almost as long as hers now. "Besides, maybe being in a family environment and having more responsibility will help keep you out of trouble. One can hope."

Tiffany wrinkled her nose at her, and Shae laughed.

❮❯

The next morning, Shae hurried down the stairs to the family parlor, a bit apprehensive. Tiffany had taken extra time to braid Shae's hair in a French braid, then looped it underneath and tied it with a rose ribbon to match the outfit. Shae dreaded being in the presence of the media, though Keith had assured her several times at dinner last night that she in no way resembled the gawky kid with braces the world remembered. Shae had just looked at him.

She nervously entered the parlor, where Keith and the man

from *Teen Planet* waited. Keith's eyes widened when he saw her, and she managed a smile. "Hi."

"Hi. You look great."

The freckle-faced stranger with the expensive camera around his neck turned from staring out the window and groaned. "Didn't you even think to discuss what you'd both be wearing? Those colors clash, and since the pictures will be in color, I must insist you wear something else," he said to Shae.

She looked down at her red blouse, uncertain, then her gaze went to Keith's burgundy shirt. She should have stuck with her first choice and not let Tiffany talk her into this.

"I'll change." Keith clipped any further comment by the photographer with a cold look toward the man. "She's perfect."

While Keith was gone, the aloof photographer introduced himself to Shae as Cameron, and said he would be doing both the write-up and taking pictures. Shae exhaled a soft breath of relief. He looked like little more than a kid and showed no sign of recognizing her.

Keith entered the room about five minutes later, wearing a navy blue cotton shirt. Cameron pulled his mouth into a wry twist. "I guess that'll have to do. Okay, first I want a picture like you two have just met. Shake hands or hug or something." He lifted his camera, looked through the viewfinder, and blew out an exasperated breath. "Can't you smile, Miss Stevens? At least look like you're glad to be with the famous Keith Travers. There's probably thousands of women wishing they were in your shoes today."

Shae gritted her teeth and offered the best smile she could under the circumstances. Keith took her hand.

Flash!

Shae sensed by the fiery glint in Keith's eyes and the hardening of his jaw that he was barely holding himself back from punching the guy's lights out.

"Perfect," Cameron announced. "Just a couple more." Flash! Flash! He clicked the camera shutter in rapid succession. "Okay, that's enough for now. Well, come on. Busy day ahead."

Keith quirked an eyebrow at Cameron's departing figure. "It appears we've been given permission to leave," he said dryly to Shae. "If the day passes without me decking that guy, I'll be surprised."

Shae chuckled. "That would make an interesting blurb for a magazine spread: 'Flash! Pop Rock Star Hammers Obnoxious Reporter With Own Camera. The Truth Exposed.' "

Keith groaned, his eyes briefly sliding shut.

Shae sobered and put a hand to his arm. "Seriously, Keith, don't worry about Cameron's behavior on my account. I've had my share of reporters in the past, and though some were nice, a lot of them were their own breed. I remember Daddy getting mad when an article would misquote something he said. And Mama never could stand it when photographers popped up out of nowhere and hounded us while we were having family time."

Keith suddenly beamed a smile so wide that Shae looked at him confused. "What? Why are you looking at me like that?"

"This is the first time I've heard you casually mention your parents since I've known you. It's a good sign." He took her hand and squeezed. "I guess we better go before Attila comes looking for us."

Shae gave a distracted nod, his words making her think. She was surprised to discover it had been easy to talk to Keith about her parents; the words had just tumbled out without her noticing them. And she wasn't sure that was such a "good sign" at all. At some point this past week she'd started considering Keith as much more than a friend. And that was dangerous. She would need to watch herself.

Tomorrow he would leave for California. And Shae would again be alone.

twelve

Outside, a dark blue luxury car awaited them. Freddie sat behind the wheel, wearing what looked like a chauffeur's uniform. Lifting her brow at the incongruous sight, Shae glanced at Keith as he opened the door to the back.

He shrugged. "Freddie rented it for the day. He also plans to be our official driver."

"But where did he get that outfit?"

"Who knows?"

As soon as the car took off, Cameron, who sat in the front passenger seat, twisted his body to face them, snapping pictures and firing questions at both Keith and Shae. Keith suggested that Cameron turn around and fasten his seat belt, since it was safer—especially with Freddie driving. Cameron gave him an incredulous look, but did face front and buckle up. However, the questions didn't stop, and Keith shook his head.

"Gotta be a rookie," he muttered so only Shae could hear.

Soon discovering that Freddie's aggressive personality matched his driving, Shae felt thankful for the one-hour reprieve they would have on the ferry. When they arrived at the mainland they drove into the old settlement of Newport, with its quaint homes and cobbled streets dating back to the colonial era, then on to Cliff Walk. Shae felt as if she'd been swept into another time. She'd visited this seaport before, but the grandeur never ceased to take her breath away.

Mansions of the millionaires, left over from the gilded age of the late nineteenth century, lay spread out along the curved, rocky coast. They went to The Breakers, the Italian Renaissance style palazzo that once belonged to the famous Vanderbilts. With its many arches, colonnades, and tall chimneys, the opulent manor sat on a sea of green lawn at the end of the stretch

139

of land. Trees sheltered three of its sides, cutting it off from the other mansions.

They entered the great hall through a curtained archway, and Shae looked up, stunned. The ceiling loomed above and had been painted to resemble a cloud-covered sky, giving the room an even greater sense of expansiveness. Everywhere one looked was intricate scrollwork, alabaster, marble, mosaics, and antique wood. The ceiling, walls, railings, pillars, furniture, chandeliers—nothing looked simple. A red-carpeted grand staircase led to spacious balconies that opened to other rooms. One wall, made mostly of glass, gave a fantastic view of the ocean waves crashing onto the rocks.

"The breakers of the ocean are what Mr. Vanderbilt named the house for—hence, The Breakers," the tour guide informed them. "The Breakers is one of the grandest mansions on Cliff Walk. Seventy rooms wrap around the great hall, the room in which we are now standing. . ."

"Imagine what the cleaning bill for a place like this would be," Keith whispered in an aside to Shae. "Millie would be set for life."

Shae giggled. The tour guide cast a curious glance her way, but continued her monologue. After their tour, they exited the manor, and Keith turned to Shae.

"How about a stroll down Cliff Walk?"

She looked over the expanse of green lawns, down the ribbon of sandy trail that went on for three miles, mansions as magnificent as The Breakers on one side of the path, the restless ocean on the other. "Maybe not, Keith. I feel kind of dizzy after all that. And besides," she shot a furtive glance Cameron's way, "somehow I don't think it would be much fun with him breathing down our necks and ordering us around, like he did in there."

Keith gave a short nod. "Okay then—how about lunch?"

"I'm game."

They piled into the car and headed for a nearby wharf and a restaurant that had been recommended to Shae. Colorful sailboats, sleek motorboats, and huge yachts and fishing boats dotted the rippling sea, which almost reflected the overcast sky and had turned a greenish gray.

Cameron took pictures of Keith and Shae while they ate at the outdoor restaurant, stopping every now and then to dig into his fried shrimp and smelts. With her fork, Shae twisted a piece of the succulent white meat from her lobster tail, dipping it into a silver salver of melted butter. "It's too bad there were no boat races today. You would have loved seeing them."

Keith looked up from his plate. "I'm from Rhode Island too, remember. I've seen quite a few boat races." His tone questioned her, sounded strange.

"Oh, yeah, right." Feeling heat rise to her face, Shae bent her head to take a bite of rice pilaf. Who could concentrate on what to say with Cameron constantly snapping pictures? He must have shot at least two rolls of film already.

On their return to Old Harbor, the sky had darkened and the sea lashed against the pilings of the dock. Shae noticed disappointment cloud Keith's features. "Looks like sailing is out."

"Maybe not," Shae murmured. "It might clear."

"Maybe. Oh, well. Ready for the shopping district? Or is that a loaded question to ask a woman?" He gave her a teasing grin.

Shae laughed. "Always."

Yet before they could head to the long line of renovated historical buildings and shops, Cameron shouted to them. "Wait! I want to get a few shots of you over there—by that yacht."

Keith barely suppressed a groan, and Shae rolled her eyes. The wind had picked up, and she could hardly see how Cameron's idea would make a good shot, but she followed Keith to the wharf. At least they weren't overly conspicuous, since tourists were scattered throughout the area, also taking pictures with their cameras. And although the sky was murky, a few others besides Keith wore sunglasses.

"Point to the yacht," Cameron instructed Keith, "as if you're explaining things to her. And you," he turned to Shae, "look up at him as if you're hanging on his every word."

Muttering something about overzealous cameramen, Keith complied. Cameron took several side shots, and Shae tried to keep her eyes open, though salt spray stung them.

"Okay," Cameron said finally, "on to the next item on the agenda."

Keith shook his head in disgust. Shae hoped this "dream date" would soon end, but on second thought maybe she didn't. Keith was leaving in the morning. This was her last day to spend in his company, and she wanted to make every minute count.

They strode the sidewalks of the shopping district, with its rows of two- and three-story brown and white historic buildings packed closely together. Cameron dogged Keith and Shae's every step. Freddie was waiting in the car, with the complaint that his bunions were hurting him. Keith shot a glance over his shoulder, then turned to Shae, mischief turning his lips up at the corners.

"Are you game to start having some real fun on this date?"

Shae nodded, wondering what he was up to.

"On the count of three." He took a few more steps, darted another glance over his shoulder. "One, two. . ." He grabbed her hand. "Three—Run!"

They dashed down the sidewalk, skirting surprised tourists and ignoring Cameron's protests behind them to stop. For the first time that day, Shae's heart felt light as she sped with Keith around the corner of a building as though they were truant children escaping an overbearing schoolmaster.

They flew through the narrow space, single file, and around the back of the store, then came along the other side. Keith peeked around the building in the direction from which they'd come.

"All clear." He scoped the area around him. "Let's duck into that ice cream shop."

They scampered to the brown brick structure, ignoring the curious stares from passersby, and hurried through the door.

Keith shot a glance out the window. "I think we lost him." He threw a boyish grin at Shae, one that she couldn't help answering with a smile of her own.

"Won't you get in trouble for this?" she asked.

"At this point, I don't care. Do you?"

"No," she admitted. "It's nice to be able to breathe again, without being told how to pose, or having to worry about embarrassing candid shots." She cocked her head with a teasing grin. "So now I guess we can add hide-and-seek to your list of games, huh?"

"Let's just hope Cameron's not that great at the seeking part." He looked beyond her to the counter. "As long as we're here—how about some ice cream?"

"Why doesn't it surprise me that you would suggest food?"

Keith laughed and bought two chocolate silk ice creams. They ate the messy treat, licking the drips along the sides of the waffle cones like two little kids. Afterward they left the shop to browse the area, all the while keeping a watch out for Cameron. At a department store, Shae pulled Keith inside, wanting to see a new line of straw hats. He patiently waited while she tried different ones on, and gave her a one-line appraisal of each.

"That one makes you look as if you're wearing a whole flower garden on your head. . . . That one looks like a flying saucer. . . . Whoever made that one must have lost his equilibrium. . . . Now, you look like you're wearing an overturned bowl sitting on a plate."

Shae rolled her eyes and pulled off the straw bonnet. She reached for the last hat, a breezy number with a wide rim and scarlet band. "Well, Mr. Fashion Expert?"

"Hmm." He smiled. "I like it."

Shae liked it too.

Hat decided on, Keith dragged Shae to the electronics section. She watched while he scanned the shelves and fiddled with the dials and buttons of the store's demo models.

"Don't you have a stereo?" she finally asked.

"Yeah, sure," Keith muttered as he switched on the Dolby sound. "But they're always coming out with something better, and I'm not against upgrading."

Shae rolled her eyes. She preferred antiques to new products. And as for any electronic gadgets she had, her motto was: If it works, keep it.

After fiddling with the stereo another minute, Keith rose. "Maybe we should look into buying you a computer while you're here. If they have them, that is. It would cut down on your workload."

"No, thanks. I'm not that electronically inclined. Besides, even if I did agree to shell out big bucks for something like that, how would we carry it out of here? On our backs?"

He grinned. "You have a point."

At the checkout, Shae pulled out her wallet, but Keith insisted on buying her the hat, to remember their day together. After leaving the store, they crossed the street to the next block when fat raindrops suddenly splattered them.

"Uh-oh," Keith muttered, turning his head up to the boiling grayish black clouds. He'd barely gotten the words out of his mouth before the sky unleashed a torrent.

"Quick, under that awning!"

Shae clapped a hand to her new bonnet and scampered with him to shelter, glad she'd rejected Tiffany's advice about the shawl and had worn her windbreaker instead. Keith linked his arm around her waist, drawing her close in the narrow space and trying to prevent rain from hitting her.

She craned her head to look up at him. His rain-darkened hair hung in dripping strands, and he futilely wiped rivulets of water from his dark lenses with two fingers, then gave up and pulled the shades off.

"Guess the sunset dinner by the ocean is off, huh?" Shae quipped softly.

Keith moved his head to look at her. "I'll make it up to you next time."

Her heart jumped. "Next time?"

"I'm coming back, Shae, you can depend on it," he said quietly. His eyes searched hers. "That is, if it's okay with you?"

She managed a nod, lost in the blue of his eyes and wishing he would kiss her.

As though reading Shae's mind, Keith moved to face her and wound his other arm around her waist. "I'm so glad your little sister sent in that contest form. It's changed my life," he whispered before dipping his head to hers.

Her heart hammering, Shae slid her arms around his neck and kissed him back while the rain beat down all around them, and her hat tumbled backward to the ground.

And she knew, beyond any doubt, she'd lost her heart to this man.

❧

Once the downpour stopped, Keith took Shae's hand and headed with her back to the rental car. A few buildings across the street they ran into Cameron, who glowered at them, his expression as forbidding as the dark skies. From his dry clothing and hair, Keith surmised he'd found shelter during the storm.

"Was that fun?" Cameron asked sarcastically.

"Much," Keith said with a grin.

"You can be certain that your manager will hear about your stunt."

"I'll save you the trouble," Keith said, his voice light. "I'll confess my crime and turn myself in. Only please don't suggest a bread and water diet."

Cameron snorted. "This is all just one big joke to you, isn't it, Travers? Well, we'll see who gets the last laugh." His voice sounded almost smug.

"What did he mean by that?" Shae whispered when he marched ahead of them.

"Who knows?" Keith shrugged, not all that worried. "How about an early dinner?"

Shae laughed. "You and your stomach."

They dined indoors on broiled sea bass, in a secluded corner away from the curious stares of others. Though Cameron kept up with his relentless photo shoot, Keith noticed that Shae seemed more relaxed. Their little breakout from Cameron must have done her some good. It certainly had done Keith good. Remembering the feel of her in his arms, he wished this date would soon end, so they could return to The Roosting Place and he could be alone with Shae to tell her what was on his heart.

At last they headed back to the inn. Freddie dropped Keith and Shae off, then took Cameron to the island's airport. The ocean's waves splashed upon the shore, and night insects began their chirring. Yellow light glowed from the windows, casting Keith and Shae in a soft pool of illumination. Before she could go inside, he grabbed her wrist.

"Stay and watch the sunset with me."

Shae's forehead wrinkled. "What sunset? The sky is gray and getting darker."

"So, we'll pretend."

She shook her head, smiling. "You really are just a big kid, aren't you?"

"Guess the secret's out. And I tried so hard to keep it."

Shae's brow arched. "Oh, yeah—speaking of secrets, you never did tell me about how you got the butter to stay on the popcorn."

Keith let out a great laugh. Shae pulled her hand from his, crossed her arms and stared.

He winked. "Family secret."

"Last time you said it was a trade secret."

"It's both. My grandpa was in the popcorn business."

"Humph." Shae turned on her heel. "I've got to check at the desk and make sure everything went smoothly while I was gone."

"Come back?" His words were low.

She paused without turning around, gave a brief nod, and hurried up the steps and through the door. Keith stuck his hands in his jacket pockets and stared at the spot where she'd been.

"Now that the dream date is over, I want you to leave my sister alone."

Tommy's grave voice sailed from a nearby copse of trees, and Keith turned in surprise. He watched as the tall man stepped out of the shadows and approached, his steps squishing in the grass.

"I'm not kidding, Travers. Just head on home to California, and don't come back."

Keith eyed him, trying to tamp his irritation. He reminded himself that with his three sisters, and in a similar situation, he might have acted the same way. "I care about Shae. I would never hurt her."

Tommy snorted. "Is that what you told the others too?" He shook his head. "You're bad news. I've heard about you and your exploits. Life has hurt Shae enough. She doesn't need a big star playboy musician making things worse."

Keith grimaced. "What makes you so sure you know just what Shae needs?"

"I may not know everything she needs, but I know for sure it isn't you!" Tommy said between clenched teeth, jabbing an accusatory finger toward Keith while spitting the last word.

"Why? Because of who your parents were? Because you don't want her to get involved in the music business like them?"

A look of perplexity crossed Tommy's features. "She told you about that?" At Keith's abrupt nod, Tommy's expression darkened. "All the more reason for you to stay away, Travers. If she's telling you her secrets, that means she's starting to trust you. And we both know what a riot that is, don't we?"

Keith ignored the sardonic words and regarded the man across from him, his gaze steady. "I love her, and I think she loves me."

"You don't even know what the word means," Tommy shot back. "And as for Shae, neither does she. This dating thing is new to her. She's got stars in her eyes concerning you, is all. Once you fade from her life, she'll forget you exist and find someone better suited to her. I guarantee it. I know my sister better than anyone."

His blood beginning to simmer, Keith turned away. "I doubt you know her at all," he muttered before heading down the road. He wasn't sure where he was going, but at this point he knew he'd better get away before he did something stupid. Like punch Shae's brother in the nose.

As he walked, the glimmer of uncertainty Tommy had lit burst into flame. Tommy *was* Shae's brother. He'd known her her whole life, so it stood to reason that he would understand her better than someone who'd known her only a short time— like Keith. Did Shae's feelings run shallow, whereas Keith's ran deep? Was getting to know Keith just a novel experience for Shae, one that she'd file away in a scrapbook of memories and later forget? Though at first she'd been a little dazed around him, she'd never acted starstruck in his company. Yet, considering her history, that didn't come as much of a surprise.

Keith didn't want a fan to love him, he wanted a woman— one who would love Keith the person, not Keith the singer. A woman like Shae. No, not a woman like Shae. Only Shae. Yet except for today's kiss, she hadn't exactly encouraged Keith concerning a relationship between them. . .and that kiss might have just been a spur-of-the-moment thing with her, a curiosity fueled by her innocence, nothing serious on her part. . .

Annoyed with himself for not being sure of the answers and irritated with Tommy for putting the questions there in the first place, Keith swiped a hand through his hair and continued down the road.

æ

Shae twisted the wrench over the nut under the handle, stopping the faucet's slow drips. One of her guests had previously called the desk, complaining about the problem, and though Shae wasn't great when it came to home improvement, she did know how to fix a leak. Besides, it was too late to call anyone else.

The relieved tourist thanked her, and Shae put the wrench

back in the toolbox and hurried to the porch, anxious to spend more time with Keith. Now that she knew he planned to return to Block Island, she wasn't as wary of him as she'd been before. He seemed to feel as deeply about her as she'd come to feel concerning him.

She opened the door and stepped outside. Tommy sat on a chair on the veranda, but there was no sign of anyone else.

"Where's Keith?" she asked.

Tommy shrugged. "He took off walking down the road."

"Just like that?" Shae looked at her brother in surprise. "Did he say where he was going?"

"No. But then guys like him usually don't. Once they get bored, or when something more interesting attracts their attention, they take off. He probably went to go check out one of the island's livelier nightclubs—one that serves alcohol."

Shae crossed her arms. "You're just prejudiced against Keith because of his profession. He quit that lifestyle—he told me so." Frowning, she stepped to the edge of the porch stairs and stared past the lawn to the road, barely discernable now that darkness had come.

"Most guys like that will say anything to get what they want," Tommy said, his voice low, "anything they think you want to hear. No, Shae. I speak from experience. You can't trust that type. I've met enough dishonest people to recognize one when I see him."

Shae thought of the many times Keith had asked her to trust him. He had seemed so sincere. And though at first she'd pushed him away, later she *had* opened her heart and trusted him with her innermost secrets, a part of herself no one knew about.

She shook her head. "No, Tommy, you're wrong about him." Her words sounded vague to her own ears.

Yet what if Tommy were right? Shae was inexperienced when it came to men. She recalled the scandalous bits of information about Keith's history she'd read in the magazine at the hospital's gift shop. But what if it wasn't just history?

What if it described his present life too?

Troubled, Shae spun around and moved toward the door. "I'm going to call it a night," she muttered, wanting to escape the doubt Tommy was feeding her mind. She needed to be alone, to try to separate the facts from the fiction.

"Night, Sis. I know it's hard for you to face the truth, but you'll get through this. You're strong."

Shae held back a wry laugh. *Strong?* Right now, she felt as if she were beginning to crumble inside.

✦

Shae awoke to a clear day, much calmer than the night's thunderstorms. A beautiful eastern sky of lilac and mauve, with splashes of pink, heralded the sun's appearance. Strange that the day promised such beauty when her heart felt as if another storm brewed inside. She took a sip of coffee and continued to stare at the secluded beach from the window of her dining nook.

"Hi. Want some company?"

The familiar voice jarred her thoughts, and she turned. Keith stood in the entrance, wearing his bomber jacket and holding his overnight bag in one hand. The sight brought a lump to her throat. "Leaving so soon?"

Nodding, he dropped the bag to the floor. "Freddie is checking us out now." He took a seat at the table.

"Oh." She toyed with the handle of her mug. "Guess you're anxious to get back to the glamour of the big city, huh?"

He shrugged. "I'll be glad to start recording that new CD, though I did enjoy taking a break away from it all." His gaze seemed to impale her. "And I imagine you'll be happy to have things back to normal after I'm gone. No more worries of some girl possibly recognizing me and creating havoc in your inn. And no one to badger you with unwanted questions about your life." He sounded almost bitter, though his tone was light.

Shae stared into her cup. "It has been an interesting experience. One I won't soon forget."

A long pause. "Neither will I."

At his low, intense words, she raised her head. His eyes seemed to question while at the same time compel her to draw closer. Confused, she averted her gaze to the window.

"Beautiful day for travel."

Keith blew out a long breath. "Shae, we need to talk."

She tightened her grip on the mug. *Here it comes. Tommy was right. He's going to tell me it was fun while it lasted, but now that his vacation is over, so are we.* Remembering Keith's words at the store about upgrading, she really shouldn't be surprised.

"I don't think there's anything left to talk about," she said hurriedly. Taking a large swig of her coffee, she scalded her tongue. "Mmm," she moaned, clapping a hand over her mouth.

"You okay?"

Shae gave a brisk nod and heard him walk to the sink, the creak of the cupboard door opening and water gurgling into a tumbler. He came to her side and hunkered down to her level, handing her the glass.

"This will help."

Shae didn't want to look at him but couldn't resist. His eyes were gentle, troubled. The crazy idea of throwing herself into his arms and begging him not to leave her flitted across her mind, but instead she focused on the glass, taking it from him.

"Thanks." She took a sip of water, holding it in her mouth a few seconds to ease her throbbing tongue, then swallowed.

"I'll never forget these past weeks with you," Keith said quietly. "Both the good times and the bad."

Shae forced down the emotion threatening to overwhelm her. His words sounded like a permanent good-bye. Well, if that's what he wanted, so be it. She forced a smile. "And I've also enjoyed your stay at our island paradise, Keith. It'll be a memory I'll long treasure. Something to tell my grandchildren someday."

He flinched and stood, gripping the edge of the table. "Then I guess there's nothing more to say."

"Guess not." Her gaze returned to her mug. The seconds ticked by, but still he didn't go. When she thought she wouldn't be able to stand the silence any longer, he spoke.

"Shae. . ."

The door opened and Freddie appeared. "There you are. Time to leave. Plane's waiting."

Shae forced herself to rise and hold out her hand for Keith to shake. "Good-bye, Keith. It was a pleasure to serve you and your manager as my guests. I wish you a safe trip and much more success."

Keith stared at her a moment, then took her hand. But instead of shaking it, he brought it to his lips and kissed the inside of her curled fingers, sending spirals of electricity swirling through her.

"Good-bye, Shae." His eyes were steady when he looked at her again. "I hope you find everything in life that makes you happy." He turned, picked up his bag and followed Freddie out the door—and out of her life. Forever.

Shae collapsed to her chair and folded her arms on the table, burying her head against them.

thirteen

Bleary-eyed, Shae tried to focus. For the second time in a row, the long column of figures didn't add up. Disgusted, she tossed her pencil next to the adding machine with a muffled exclamation. The past two weeks, she'd thrown herself into her work, doing as much as she could to keep her mind off her problems. As a result, her concentration was wearing thin. If that wasn't bad enough, the nightmares were almost a nocturnal ritual now, and Keith had been transported into them too.

"Shae?" Katie poked her head in the office. "Got a minute? Pastor Williams is here to see you."

"Pastor Williams?" Shae said in surprise. She threw a disparaging glance at the aggravating book work and rose from her chair. "Sure. I'll be right there."

He stood in the lobby, his hazel eyes brightening when he saw her. "It's good to see you again, Shae. Is there someplace we can go to talk?"

Curious, she nodded and led him to the front parlor. He took a seat on the sofa, declining her offer of refreshment, and she sat across from him in an antique chair she'd recently acquired.

"How have you been?" he asked. "I know things have been rough for you now that Tiffany's gone to live with your brother."

Shae nodded. "Yes, even with tourist season at its peak the days seem quiet without her. But I'm holding out. I did find a new permanent act for the floor show, so that's a burden removed." She looked at her hands. "Hillary decided to stay on the mainland near Robert and see him through this. He's still in a coma, you know."

"I know. I visited the hospital yesterday." He hesitated.

"Have you heard from Keith?"

Her head shot up. "No. Why should I have?"

His expression was puzzled. "Well, I thought. . . You know he came to see me the night before he left, don't you?"

Shae's heart tripped. "No, I didn't. What about?"

A gentle smile lit his face. "Sorry, Shae. That's confidential. But he did suggest I visit you after he'd gone." Shae averted her gaze, and his words became quiet. "Actually, I'd already planned to, but my schedule has been so full. Then when you didn't show up for church services twice in a row, I grew concerned and shuffled my appointments around to come today."

Shae nodded, looking at her hands. "Did he tell you everything about me?" Her voice was bitter, resigned.

"No. But he did hint that you might have something you want to discuss."

Shae's gaze lifted to Pastor Williams. With his boyish features and earnest smile, this dark-haired man looked too young to be in the ministry. But his anointed messages had touched many lives, and she knew God had called him to this vocation. She swallowed, knowing it was time.

"He's right. There is something I want to share with you." And over the next ten minutes, she told him everything, about the dreams, about her identity, about her guilt. After she finished, he studied her, a hint of sorrow and concern clouding his eyes. He seemed to think a moment.

"Shae, do you have a Bible handy?"

"I think I have one in here." She located a pocket-sized New Testament in the drawer of the end table beside her. "How's this?"

"Perfect." He thumbed through the pages. "Listen to this. It's from Romans 8: 'Therefore, there is now no condemnation for those who are in Christ Jesus, because through Christ Jesus the law of the Spirit of life set me free from the law of sin and death.' " He looked at her. "God is greater than the condemnation you feel in your heart, Shae. He knows you didn't mean those things you said to your parents, and He doesn't want you to remain in bondage to guilt for past mistakes."

"But if I hadn't been such a rebel and they hadn't changed their plans to spend more time with me, they would still be alive today," she insisted.

"How do you know that?"

"What?" Shae blinked, startled by the unexpected question.

"How do you know when the time would have come for them to meet their maker?" He stroked his jaw in thought when she remained silent. "Tell me, Shae, did you force your parents to change their travel plans?"

"Of course not. I was just a kid. I didn't have that kind of power over them."

"Exactly. They made their own choices."

She looked down. "But I screamed horrible words at them. I said I wished they were dead. . .and, then they were."

He squeezed her hand. "Shae, you didn't cause that airplane to crash. You don't have that kind of power either. Don't get me wrong, the words we speak are important and powerful— but do you really think an all-loving God would allow the temper tantrum of an immature sixteen year old to be the weapon that took His children?"

"When you say it that way, it sounds silly," Shae admitted, uncertain. "But why did they have to die? Why like that? They were good people who loved and served God."

Removing his hand, the pastor leaned back against the cushion and let out a long breath. "We don't understand everything, Shae. Our finite minds don't have the capacity to grasp it all— though God does often reveal His truths to us. And we do know there is a devil who steals from God's children, if given the chance. Yet we have to go on trusting God, who knows all, to be God, and we must hold fast to our faith in Him."

Shae released a weary sigh. "I understand all you're saying, Pastor, but I still find it hard to believe God could love me, though I try to be a Christian and do good things to make up for that day."

"Oh, Shae. No matter how many brownie points you try to chalk up to earn your way into heaven, it's an impossible task. If we could earn our way there, then Jesus wouldn't have had to die. He took every sin—every terrible thing Marcia Shae Stevens ever did or will do—to the cross with Him. Accept His grace, Shae. God is all-loving—He isn't able to be anything else. And He's all-forgiving. He doesn't hold the past against you. You are forgiven. Now you need to let go of it and forgive yourself.

"The forty-third chapter of Isaiah says He blots out your transgressions and won't remember your sins anymore. Shae, once you tell God you're sorry, He doesn't even remember what you did."

She attempted a smile, but it fell short and tears clouded her eyes instead. "I wish I could believe you, Pastor. I really do. . . ."

He looked directly into her eyes. "I'd like you to come in for counseling."

"Counseling?" She bit her lip. "For how long?"

"Until we get to the root of the problem," he answered without hesitancy. "It might take weeks—even months. But if I felt it wasn't important, I wouldn't have suggested it."

She nodded. "Okay, if you think it will help."

"I don't *think* it will help, Shae. I *know* it will. You need to learn who you are in Christ—to reprogram your mind to God's way of thinking. Marcia Shae Stevens is very special to God. There's no one else like her in His eyes."

His soft, emphatic words unleashed several tears, and they rolled down her cheeks.

He patted her hand. "I want you to read the entire chapter of 1 John before you come. It's often called the love chapter." He smiled. "Soon you'll see why."

❧

Shae sat in her dining nook, sipping her coffee. Katie walked in, a magazine in her hands, a wary look in her eyes. "Seen the new issue of *Teen Planet*?"

Shae shook her head. "Is it out?"

"Yeah, you could say that." The young girl dropped the magazine in front of Shae and left the room. Shae studied the doorway where she'd exited. Katie seemed edgy, and Shae was sure it had something to do with what was inside the glossy pages.

Taking a steadying breath, she flipped through the magazine until she found the spread. Her heart lurched at the photos of her and Keith together at The Breakers, on the ferry, at the restaurant, by the yacht—bringing back vivid memories of that day. With a bittersweet smile, she lightly swept a finger down his face. She turned the page and her heart stopped.

There, in a full-color three-by-five shot, stood Shae and Keith, their arms wrapped around each other, kissing beneath the awning. Underneath the photo was the caption: "Is Dream Date New Love Interest?"

Closing her eyes, Shae groaned and pushed the magazine away. Now she understood Cameron's smug comment about getting the last laugh. And she *would* be the laughingstock of the island—especially when it was discovered that Keith dumped her the next day. Shae didn't think she could stand to read the article.

She was halfway through the article when the phone rang. Her eyes on the print, Shae reached for the wall and groped for the receiver. "Hello?" she mumbled.

"Happy birthday, Sis!"

"Tommy?"

"Who else?" he said, amusement evident in his tone. "We wanted to come and see you, but Linda wasn't feeling well."

Shae pushed the magazine away. "How's she doing?"

"Some days are better than most. How are your headaches?"

"Haven't had one in weeks," she said with a grateful smile.

"Hi, Shae! Happy birthday. Did you see the new issue of *Teen Planet*?" Tiffany's voice came clearly over the line.

"Tiff! It's so good to hear your voice."

"But did you see it?"

Shae heaved a sigh. "Yeah, I saw."

"Wow! That must have been some date," Tiffany said.

"So, what are you doing for your birthday?" Tommy quickly interrupted.

"Actually, I'd forgotten it was my birthday."

"What—you're kidding!" This from Tiffany.

"Listen, Shae, I won't have this," Tommy said. "Not at all. Take the day off and have some fun. Tiffany had a great idea earlier. You always did like the gardens in Portsmouth."

Shae bunched her brows. "Why should I go all the way to Portsmouth when I live in the middle of a vacation paradise?"

"True. But you need to get off that island sometimes. Now is as good a day as any."

Shae nodded, thoughtful. Maybe her brother was right.

"Well, we'd better let you go. Phone rates, you know."

"Tommy, can I talk to Shae a minute?"

"Well, all right. Make it short. Bye, Shae."

A click, then, "Shae?"

"I'm here, Tiffany. What did you want to talk about?"

There was a pause. When Tiffany finally spoke, her voice was soft. "Thank you for sending me Mama's angel. I promise every time I look at it, I'll remember that God and His angels are watching over our family and keeping us together, even though we're apart—just like your note said."

Happy tears filled Shae's eyes. "You're more than welcome, Tiff. I love you, Kiddo."

"Love you too. . .oh, and Shae, one more thing. Um. . . If Tommy tells you anything about me dying the neighbor's poodle neon blue—it really wasn't my fault. The stupid dog stepped in a pan of paint. Honest!"

Shae laughed—she couldn't help herself. "I'll remember that."

She hung up, feeling much better. Her gaze went out the window, to the sunny day. Maybe a trip to the gardens was in order. It would be fun to do something different, and she hadn't been there in years. Katie could take care of the desk, and Shae had hired a new assistant to help out during the busy season too.

Making her decision, she grabbed the magazine and went

to her room to get her keys, first stuffing the magazine in the bottom of her bureau drawer. Though what had been written was pure garbage, she just couldn't throw away photographs of their day together.

୬

Shae ambled down the meandering path, hands in her windbreaker pockets, and enjoyed the breezy day. Everywhere she looked, a green, prickly animal stared back amid the trees. She had always loved the gardens and marveled at the skill of the person who'd crafted these amazing sculptures from greenery. Her gaze lifted to a tall cone-shaped boxwood, pruned to represent a spiral, and she smiled, watching as a cardinal landed on top.

Strolling past bushes resembling a bear, an elephant, and other animals and geometric shapes, she allowed her mind to wander to Keith—as it did most of the time now. Where was he? What was he doing? Did he ever think about her?

Shae thought over the weeks they'd shared. At first, she had to admit, she'd been a little starstruck around Keith, even if she had been somewhat of a celebrity once too. Yet at some point, the giddy feeling disappeared, and love took over. Not the superficial love a girl has for someone who is popular, attractive, and fun to be with. But the genuine love one has for another—knowing and understanding his faults, yet accepting and loving him, regardless.

And he has his share of faults, Shae thought, with a grim little smile. By no stretch of the imagination could Keith Travers be labeled perfect. He was entirely too pushy, too nosy, and too stubborn. And yet if he'd never walked into her life she might still be in hiding, beaten down by fear and guilt. For his persistence, she was grateful, though she hadn't been at the time.

Shae continued to stare up at the bush sheared to resemble a giraffe. Her smile turned dreamy when she thought of Keith's good qualities, his sensitivity, his boyish charm. . .but wait. Why was she doing this to herself? He was gone from her life—all the way across the country—and Shae hadn't heard from him once these past two months, not that she'd expected to. She had obviously only been a curiosity to Keith, a mystery—which, once it was solved, no longer appealed. Besides, as far as she knew, he hadn't recommitted his life to God. And she could never get serious about a man who didn't serve and love the Lord like she now did. She didn't want the same problems Hillary faced.

Shae forced herself to erect a wall around her heart and block out any emotions concerning Keith. Mentally she kicked herself for sightlessly staring at the animal-shaped bush for the past five minutes while daydreaming about him.

"It's over. Done with," she firmly told the green giraffe while crossing her wrists and swooping her hands flat out to the sides in a completion sign. "He's out of my life for good, and it's time to go on."

"Do you always talk to the shrubbery?"

A silent bomb exploded inside Shae's head when she heard the low words behind her. It couldn't be. Her imaginings must have gone a step further, and now she was hearing voices. She turned, dazed.

He pushed a hand through his hair, sweeping it from his forehead. The usual pair of designer sunglasses covered his eyes, but she could almost imagine their riveting blue gaze on her now.

"Keith," she managed in a breathy whisper.

"Is that all the welcome I get?" His tone was light, though he sounded uncertain. "Of course, after hearing you talk to your woodland friend here, I guess I shouldn't be surprised. I assume you were talking about me?"

She gave a slight nod, her heart pounding.

Keith let out a weary sigh. "Shae, we need to talk."

He was right. There was so much left unexplained. "Okay. There's a bench over there." She led the way, needing to sit down before she fell down.

"Actually, I was hoping for someplace more private. Like

the inn," he said, taking a seat beside her.

She studied the nearly deserted gardens and raised her brows in confusion. "Private? I don't see anyone around."

Nodding toward the bushes surrounding them, Keith gave a wry grin. "It's been said the walls have ears. I wonder if that saying applies to bushes shaped like animals too. Especially after hearing you talk to one."

Heat flashed to her face, and she lifted her chin. "Exactly how long were you watching me?"

"Long enough."

Her stomach gave a little flip. "But. . .how did you find me? How did you know I was here?"

"When my plane landed on the mainland, I called the inn." He paused. "I've missed you, Shae."

She averted her gaze, didn't respond.

"Did you miss me? Even a little?"

A small girl with a red balloon barreled around the corner and scurried down the path past them, laughing and squealing while her harried mother ran after in hot pursuit with a toddler in her arms. Keith blew out a loud breath, obviously frustrated at the interruption.

"Okay. Maybe we should go to the inn," Shae relented. "Did you drive to the gardens?"

"I took a taxi, hoping for a ride back with you."

"Actually, I splurged and took a taxi too. No room for my car on the ferry."

Keith stood and extended his hand. "Shall we?"

Shae allowed him to help her up, but once she was on her feet, she pulled her hand from his. Keith stared but didn't say a word.

In the back of the cab, he filled in the time talking of inconsequential things. Remembering their last taxi ride together, Shae was glad the conversation wasn't personal, but still she wondered what Keith had to tell her that would bring him back to the island.

Once they boarded the ferry, Shae could no longer hold

back her curiosity. "So, tell me. Why are you here?"

He stared out at the sea a long time before answering. "I was hoping you wouldn't have to ask that question."

Shae's heart gave a jolt. What did that mean? That he didn't want her to know his business? She looked out over the ocean. "Did Freddie come with you?"

"No. We've parted ways."

Shae's eyes widened as she swung her gaze to him. He continued to study the sea. "How come?" she asked.

"Let's just say we didn't see eye to eye. After a great deal of soul-searching, I chose not to renew my contract."

Shae didn't move a muscle, didn't even breathe. What was he saying?

"I've had a lot of questions," Keith mused. "I talked to Pastor Williams before I left the island last time. He cleared up a lot of things for me. Did he come see you?" He glanced her way.

She nodded. "He mentioned you came to see him, but he wouldn't tell me what you talked about."

Keith hesitated. "I was having a hard time believing God could forgive me for those years I turned away from Him. Choosing to live in a life of sin, even though I'd been raised otherwise."

"And?"

His mouth lifted in a wry grin. "And Pastor Williams pointed out the story of the prodigal son, among other things. But I still struggled with the issue. A month ago, I went to God and laid it all on the line. I told Him I was a worthless sinner who knew better than to sin, but had done it anyway. And I told Him if He still wanted me, He could have me."

Shae only stared.

Keith looked her way and chuckled. "Surprised?"

She gave a slight nod, then shook her head no. Keith laughed again.

"What about your singing?"

"I've quit the secular music business, Shae. I see now it was pulling me down."

Shae blinked, trying to absorb it all. "But. . .what will you do now?"

"I guess a lot of that depends on you."

"What do you mean?" she asked, her voice a little breathless.

"We'll talk about it more when we get to the inn."

She opened her mouth to speak, but he laid a finger alongside her lips, shaking his head. "Patience, Shae."

❧

To Shae, it seemed to take forever to reach The Roosting Place. Once there, Keith put a hand to her elbow, stopping her from going inside. Curious, she looked up at him. He smiled secretly and escorted her around to the back of the inn, to the secluded beach beside the ocean.

Shae gaped, blinked.

A table had been set on the sand, replete with a melon-colored tablecloth, silver, and china. Two chairs sat opposite one another. In the background, the cobalt blue ocean sluggishly lapped against the beach, and overhead, the sky shone turquoise.

"Happy birthday," Keith said softly.

Shae swallowed hard, tears springing to her eyes. "How. . .?"

"Tiffany managed to get ahold of me a couple of weeks ago, and we set this up. Katie helped."

She put a hand to her mouth, overwhelmed. Keith gently steered her to a chair and held it out while she slid onto it. "You did all this for me?" she managed to squeak.

Keith smiled as he took the place across from her. "Of course. And I'd do it again just to see that look on your face."

Shae offered him a wavery smile, still feeling as if she were dreaming. From the back door, Gretta suddenly appeared bearing a platter and a wide smile. *"Alles Gute zum Geburtstag, Fräulein* Stevens—a happy birthday."

"Thank you, Gretta. And thank you for the part you played in this."

Gretta blushed, the tips of her ears going red. "You enjoy this birthday dinner, *ja?"* She set two bowls of what looked like cream of celery soup on the table. "I will be back with more."

Before they began, Keith took Shae's hands and offered a blessing for the food, also asking God to bless Shae on her birthday. His fluent prayer sounded nothing like the rough one he'd stumbled through months ago when he'd cooked dinner for her.

A delicious meal of baked bluefish stuffed with dill cheese, along with buttered peas, baby carrots, and green salad followed. Throughout the dinner, Keith kept the conversation light, and though Shae would have liked to know what he meant by his last remark on the ferry, she tried her best to exhibit the patience for which he'd asked.

Taking her last bite of chocolate nut parfait, Shae let her eyes slide shut at the delightful mixture of walnuts, creamy chocolate, and vanilla cookie crumbs. "Better than any birthday cake," she said, her mouth half full.

Keith smiled. "I'm glad you enjoyed the meal. Take a walk with me along the beach?"

Shae nodded, tossing her napkin to the table. She pulled off her sandals, holding them in one hand. They plodded through the sand, side by side, but not touching. In the waning light, the gulls cawed to one another, playing games of swooping and diving. The ocean whispered its secrets, as it sloshed against the shore at rapid intervals. The wonderful smells of wildflowers and saltwater filled her senses.

"Shae, I have a proposition for you," Keith said at last.

She tensed. *A proposition?*

"As I told you, I've left the secular music industry for good. And now I want to try getting into the Christian music world—with you. Ever since we sang the duet at the inn, I've felt we should pair up. We'd make a great team. I'd write the songs, and together we'd sing them."

Shae considered a long moment. "My immediate response would be to say no—after having come from that kind of life and losing my parents to it. But I promise I *will* consider it and pray about it, Keith. If that's what God wants me to do—sing for Him—then I'm willing."

He halted and turned to face her. "Really?" His tone sounded as though he hadn't expected her to come that close to agreeing.

She nodded, smiling. "Really. Pastor Williams has been counseling with me. Through him and the sessions, God has delivered me from the fear I've had. I know now I belong to Him—really belong to Him. In fact, God never left me. I'm the one who walked away."

Shae tilted her head in thought as she stared up at his dazed expression. "I guess we both did the same thing, Keith. You walked away from God physically, and I walked away from Him emotionally. But like you, I've come home. And I'm no longer afraid for the world to find out who I am—" She broke off as Keith pulled her to him and hugged her hard.

"Oh, Shae, I'm so glad," he breathed into her hair. "I'm proud of you—that you've shown courage to deal with the past."

She nodded, barely able to breathe because he was holding her so tightly. Yet it felt wonderful to be in his arms again. He loosened his hold and looked down at her.

"I have one more surprise." He grinned. "I seem to remember promising you a sunset. I can't think of a better place than New Harbor. Come with me?"

She smiled. "I'd like that."

They drove the few miles across the island to its west side where the Great Salt Pond was located. Keith removed his sunglasses, came around to her door, and helped her out. "I know the deal was a sunset dinner by the ocean, but I didn't see how we'd drag the table over here."

Shae laughed. "Don't worry about it, Keith. This is fine."

Together they walked to the dock. Soon, a horizontal flame of red mixed with orange slashed the sky directly above the horizon, a dark band of clouds above it. Myriad boats dotted the harbor, their black silhouettes identical in color to the surrounding land. The calm sea acted as a mirror for the sky, shimmering crimson.

"It's beautiful," Shae murmured, awed with their creator.

"I have a birthday present for you," Keith said, gaining her attention.

Shae turned to him, surprised. "Another one?"

"Yeah, only this one is just from me." He held out his fists at chest level, pointing them downward. "Which hand?"

She chuckled at his endless games and tapped his right hand.

"Nope. Guess again."

Grinning, she shook her head, and tapped the other. He turned his hand upward and opened it. A piece of saltwater taffy lay in his palm.

"Oh, my favorite!" she enthused, grabbing the treat. She tore off the wax paper, stuffed it into her pocket, and popped the pink candy into her mouth.

"Okay, now try the other hand," he said when she'd finished the sweet.

"Keith, if you don't stop feeding me, you're going to make me fat," she complained. "I gained five pounds when you were here last time."

"That's okay. I'll still love you."

Her heart jumped, but she tried not to make much of his light words. It was all part of the banter, she reminded herself.

"Go on. Try the other one."

She rolled her eyes and tapped his right hand. Keith turned it over and opened his fingers. A diamond solitaire sat in his palm.

Shae only stared, unable to think, unable to form words, unable to breathe.

"Marry me, Shae," he said quietly. "Make my life complete."

When she didn't answer right away, he continued. "Now that I've found God again, my life has improved. But I still lack something. Someone with whom I can share life's joys and sorrows. Someone I can love. I want you to be that someone, Shae. . .I feel as if I've waited for you a lifetime. Marry me—tomorrow, this weekend. Whenever you say—only please make it soon."

With trembling fingers, Shae tentatively touched the ring in his hand, then turned her eyes upward to his. "Oh, Keith. . .I do love you."

His brows bunched in an anxious frown. "But?"

"But I can't marry you that soon. We've both recently recommitted our lives to God. We need time to get to know Him again, as well as taking the time to learn more about each other. Until today, I wasn't sure if I'd ever see you again."

Keith stared down at the solitaire for a moment, then looked up at her. "Will you still wear my ring?"

Shae laughed. "Of course I will. I didn't say I wouldn't marry you—just not yet."

"So is that a yes?"

She nodded, a wide smile on her face. "Yes."

Grinning, he picked up the solitaire and with infinite care slid it onto her third finger. He bent his head and kissed her slowly, sending pleasurable heat tingling through her, and she wrapped her arms around his neck.

"Though my first inclination is to try to persuade you to change your mind and marry me the first chance we get," he said quietly after pulling away a fraction, "you're right. You're one smart woman, Marcia Shae Stevens."

His hand lifted to the side of her face, his fingers slipping beneath her hair. "Only promise me one thing, okay?"

"What?"

"The exact moment you know when the time is right, let me in on it?"

Shae smiled. "Believe me, Keith, you'll be the first to know."

He gave her another melting kiss before they turned and watched the last of the sunset.

epilogue

The evening was hot, the skies shimmering a pale robin's egg blue. A crowd of thousands cheered, standing in front of an outdoor stage, where a band had just exited after playing their last song. Wearing a huge smile, a scrawny man with wild red hair and freckles approached the microphone and signaled for silence. The noise died down.

"We have a treat for you," he said into the mike. "I'm sure you've heard of Keith Travers and Marcia Stevens—the daughter of famous gospel singers Trey and Marilyn Stevens. Well, they're with us tonight, and have agreed to sing a few songs. . . ."

Backstage, Shae straightened her airy, eyelet blouse, making sure it was properly fastened and none of the buttons had popped open. The waistband of her silky broomstick skirt felt tight too. When she'd last checked the scales, they'd shown she'd put on a whopping ten pounds! She would have to force herself to moderate her food—even if she had to chain the refrigerator door shut. And definitely no more of the sweets Keith loved to share with her.

Feeling uncomfortable, Shae wished for the hundredth time that she'd bought new clothes—some that fit. The last thing she wanted to do right now was to go onstage in front of all those people. How did she ever let Keith talk her into this? She gave a wry grin. She'd always been a sucker for those mesmerizing eyes of his, and the feel of his warm hands and kisses made her melt every time. . . . Okay, so she knew how he'd talked her into it. But could she go through with the performance?

Tightening her hold on the full glass of lemon water, Shae anxiously studied the raised platform where the announcer was finishing up their introduction. Keith came up behind her, looping his arms around her waist. "Hey there, Gorgeous. Feeling okay?"

"No, I'm terrified. I've never sung for a crowd this size."

"I understand. I get that queasy feeling too. You'll do fine. Otherwise okay?"

She nodded. He took the glass from her hand and set it down, then brushed a quick kiss over her lips.

"It gives me great pleasure to introduce the new singing team of Keith Travers and Marcia Shae Stevens!"

Hearing their cue, Keith and Shae took the steps leading to the platform and sat on stools a roadie had put center stage. Keith held his guitar ready, the only accompaniment they had since the rest of their band wasn't with them. He gave her a reassuring wink as they waited for the applause to die down.

Shae's hands were clammy, and her heart raced. She looked out over the crowd and up into the sky, where pinpoints of white stars were barely visible.

"For you, Mama and Daddy," she whispered. "I love you."

Together, she and Keith sang the title song from their new CD that had topped the charts only two weeks after its release. The same song that her father had written and her parents had sung over a decade ago:

Though the road before me is long and winding,
And the way lay covered in snares,
Though the path is full of potholes,
And my life's loaded with worries and cares,
Though it seems like the night's never-ending,
And I'll never again see the dawn,
I look up and remember God's promise,
That He'll never leave me alone.

And He sends His angels to watch over us,
To guard us, protect us, help us, uphold us
And I know, no matter how bad it seems,

The heavenly troops are under His command.
Though the way is littered with broken promises,
From those who aren't perfect—like me,
Though detours sometimes lure me astray,
From the narrow path where I always should be,
Though sometimes the way I choose is rocky,
And I fall on my face in shame,
He'll always be there to turn back to,
And He'll never turn me away.

So if I stick to the road before me,
No matter how hard it may be,
I'm assured at the end He will be there,
And His heavenly Kingdom I'll see,
Then I'll look back on the road I had chosen,
Two sets of footprints making it clear,
That He never left or forgot me,
But He walked with me and always stayed near.

So if you, too, are weary,
Of the long road we all must take,
I want to encourage you, friend,
The rewards are well worth the wait,
And when the road seems too steep to climb,
Just look up and see the cross,
For He's already taken your burdens,
And He has paid the final cost.
(© 1998 PMG)

Before the final notes died away, thunderous applause filled the outdoor arena in Dallas, Texas, where several Christian bands had gathered to hold a summer music festival. Shae opened teary eyes and smiled at Keith, who gave her a soft wink. Mentally, she prepared for the next number. Keith faced the crowd, holding up his hand to get their attention.

Suspicious, Shae studied him. Now what was he up to?

"I just want to thank you for your support," he said when the noise died down. His voice amplified over the huge outdoor speakers. "That song means a lot to both of us."

He sent a glance Shae's way and smiled before turning back to the audience. "God has blessed me with a partner like Marcia. And before we sing our next song, I want to share something with all of you. Something I just found out today. . ."

Alarmed, Shae shook her head, trying to catch his eye. Keith paid no attention.

"I'm going to be a father!"

A few seconds of silence—then the buzz of murmured conversation filled the arena as people turned to their neighbors. But no one smiled. Keith looked at Shae, his brows raised in question.

Thoroughly exasperated with him, she rolled her eyes. "Well, you've told them that much. Now, you'd better tell them the rest before they start throwing things at us. Like rotten tomatoes."

Understanding dawned, and he grinned. "Maybe I should let them stew awhile. Get it? Stewed tomatoes?"

"Ke–eith!" Shae groaned softly, though she couldn't help but smile.

He chuckled and turned back to the microphone. "Did I forget to mention we were secretly married three months ago?"

At this announcement, the crowd went wild.

Keith threw Shae a sheepish grin, and she shook her head. "I can't believe you did that—though knowing you, I guess I shouldn't be surprised." Her words came soft, so the microphone wouldn't pick them up, though with the loud applause, she doubted anyone would hear.

He reached for her hand. "I'm sorry, Shae, I know we'd agreed to release the wedding announcement to the press next week. But I just had to tell someone about the baby. Am I forgiven?"

A hint of mischief tilted her lips. "Only if you tell me how you got the butter to stay on the popcorn."

Keith let out a great laugh and pulled her to him. "I love you, Marcia Shae Travers. You are definitely the woman for me!"

He kissed her while the crowd sent up another roar of approval, and Shae forgot all about buttered popcorn.

A Letter To Our Readers

Dear Reader:

In order that we might better contribute to your reading enjoyment, we would appreciate your taking a few minutes to respond to the following questions. We welcome your comments and read each form and letter we receive. When completed, please return to the following:

Rebecca Germany, Fiction Editor
Heartsong Presents
PO Box 719
Uhrichsville, Ohio 44683

1. Did you enjoy reading *Angels to Watch Over Me* by Pamela Griffin?

   ❑ Very much! I would like to see more books by this author!

   ❑ Moderately. I would have enjoyed it more if

   _____

   _____

2. Are you a member of **Heartsong Presents**?   Yes ❑ No ❑
   If no, where did you purchase this book?_____

   _____

3. How would you rate, on a scale from 1 (poor) to 5 (superior), the cover design?_____

4. On a scale from 1 (poor) to 10 (superior), please rate the following elements.

   _____ Heroine   _____ Plot

   _____ Hero   _____ Inspirational theme

   _____ Setting   _____ Secondary characters

5. These characters were special because_____
    _____
    _____

6. How has this book inspired your life?_____
    _____
    _____

7. What settings would you like to see covered in future
    Heartsong Presents books?_____
    _____
    _____

8. What are some inspirational themes you would like to see
    treated in future books?_____
    _____
    _____

9. Would you be interested in reading other **Heartsong
    Presents** titles?   Yes ❏   No ❏

10. Please check your age range:
    ❏ Under 18   ❏ 18-24   ❏ 25-34
    ❏ 35-45   ❏ 46-55   ❏ Over 55

Name _____

Occupation _____

Address _____

City _____ State _____ Zip _____

Email _____